TIM BENNETT

SALT

for the Supper Table

TIM BENNETT

SALT
for the Supper Table

ELIM
EP
PUBLISHING

ISBN #0-9713711-1-3

Cover design and page layout: David G. Danglis / Pinwheel Creative
Cover cartoon: Joe Glisson

Published by: Elim Publishing
                  1679 Dalton Road
                  Lima, NY 14485

*This book is dedicated to my family
without whom most of this book
would never have been written:
my wife, Véronique,
my daughter, Alicia,
and my two sons,
Samuel and Jonathan.*

*Special thanks to God
for the major blessing they are in my life.
I love you all.*

Acknowledgments

I would like to first thank Jesus, my Lord and Savior, for His timely encouragements to keep me writing, without whom I would have thrown in the writing towel a long time ago.

I also want to thank my wife, Véronique, for her support and prayers throughout this project.

A word of appreciation must also go to the talented Joe Glisson for the cover cartoon, Dave Danglis for his excellent layout and editorial suggestions, and Elim Publishing for their pioneering venture into digital publishing. Their desire to assist Elim missionaries in publishing their own books is truly a wonderful idea.

Merci beaucoup tout le monde!

Contents

"Let your conversation be always full of grace,
seasoned with salt,
so that you know how to answer everyone."
(Colossians 4:6)

Preface

The following book was born out of comments made by readers of my first book, **With A Grain of Salt.** Although I did not consciously write that book with families in mind (it is a collection of humorous and inspirational stories both fiction and non-fiction), some readers used it as a devotional around the supper table to the delight of all. With that kind of positive response and encouragement from families I thought: *why not put together a collection of articles that would appeal to this readership and also include some questions and projects related to the theme of the story?* Most of the stories come directly from my life but there are also some historical, humorous, and serious pieces as well. I've also included one short story, *Don't Go Gently Into That Good Night,* because I thought it creatively brings home the threat of the euthanasia movement. (Please do not interpret this as an anti-cosmetic saleswoman story. To focus solely on your career and goals and becoming desensitized to others can happen in any profession.) All the stories are meant to serve as launching pads for personal sharing and discussion around the Bible as well as a challenge to apply the Word of God to your daily life, and the life of your family. As you will soon discover, our family is much like yours, imperfect, but we are pressing upward to that higher calling that we all have in Jesus Christ with faith and hope. My prayer is that this book will help you and your family to do the same.

Getting a Dog
and Counting the Cost

Let's just say I forgot. My wife, Véronique, and I told the kids we could not have a dog until *"after"* we owned a house. After we moved into the house Véronique tried, *"after"* we got settled. A year later we were running out of *"afters"* and we both knew our days were numbered.

Yet, although Véronique didn't crave canine contact because of the messes, I had to admit, I really wanted a dog again. When I was ten, my puppy, Princess, got hit by a car and I hadn't loved a dog since. I was willing to try again and also let the kids enjoy the experience with me.

But, like I said, I forgot. I forgot that dogs require a lot of time. Time to train them . . . clean up after them . . . feed them . . . walk them. Yes, it's therapeutic having a creature jumping and wriggling for joy to see you every morning but it gets old especially when he summons you a half hour before the alarm clock.

A visionary teenage girl told me: "He's cute now but it's too bad they are not as cute when they get big." At first I interpreted her comments as jealousy, since her family never had a dog. Then one day I saw a dog that looked like an older Skip and I grimaced. He had Skip's fur coloring and he was ransacking a paper bag left on the street. He was skinny, dirty, and—truth be told—not a sculptural masterpiece. I wondered if I could love Skip if he developed a disproportionate body like that. Was my love based on his "cuteness" or a commitment? Had I really counted the cost?

I guess the real test came when Skip went from being an adorable puppy to a mischievous teenager in 60 days. I hadn't realized big dogs (he's a Lab and German Shepherd mix) don't stay small for long. In the early days, I would call "Skip Watches" where we would all gather around the little fella to see what he would do. I marvelled at how fully he could relax on his stomach with his head between his front legs stretched to the limit and his hind legs just as extended in the opposite direction.

I also noticed how content he was with simple pleasures like chewing on a stick for hours. I would smile, too, watching him from behind. His legs were bowed and he resembled a cowboy who'd been riding a bull too long as he ambled off to his next adventure. Other times he'd make me laugh as he tried to stop insects from crawling on his turf.

Now, only five months later, Skip is big. His ears are approaching my waist. His mostly black head is nobly shaped with dashes of brown for eyebrows and peanut butter colored lower jaws. The same color also marks his legs with some splotches of white on his broad chest. He is majestically well-proportioned and the black fur on his back glistens in the sun.

Despite his regal appearance, however, he takes great joy in working with his paws—a third of our backyard is now a barren wasteland with multiple craters from his excavating projects. It makes me wonder if he buried a bone somewhere and just forgot where he put it. He has also attacked the soft dirt in the flowerpots on the terrace more than once and chewed on everything he could get his mouth around. His little yelping has changed to a deep baritone implying imperial commands. When I give him his food he sucks it up in 30 seconds and then looks at me like, "Hey, that's great for an appetizer but where's the all-you-can-eat buffet?"

Did I count the cost? No. Do the kids love him? Yes. Would I do it again knowing the time involved? Probably. After all, God did use animals in the life of King David to prepare him to rule and Solomon wrote: *"A righteous man cares for the needs of his animal"* (Proverbs 12:10).

Other verses to look up: **1 Samuel 17:15, 20, 28, 33-37**

Questions:

What are some of the things David learned by taking care of his father's sheep?

What did David's older brother accuse him of? Was it true?

Are you exemplifying these same qualities David had with your animals? (Assuming you have some, of course.)

What are some things you can learn by taking care of animals?

Young Kids Can Keep Us Humble

I think my three children are wonderful except when they are misbehaving. At these times, I must confess, in my eyes, they fall far short of the wonder to which they are called. Yet, in my more serene moments, I see all of them as major blessings and small instruments of God to keep me humble.

Just for clarification, humility is not to be equated with I-am-a-door-mat-ism or I-am-a-worm-ism. These are just other faces of pride in reverse, which can be as nauseating to others as seeing yourself as superior.

Humility, according to the Bible, is seeing yourself as significant and valuable in the sight of God—no better nor less than anyone else.

One of the major things I've learned through my children, however, is how much I do not know and how incompetent I am to raise them successfully without divine help. I often find myself looking to God for a stable view of myself because their perception of me keeps changing. One second I seem to be their hero and the next I hear: "You don't know anything, Dad!"

Young boys also have a tendency to magnify the strengths of their fathers, which can lead to some humbling moments. They don't realize that it's one thing to scare away the imaginary bogeyman in the closet and quite another to tackle a real thief coming through the window. Most dads don't want their sons to know that they may have trouble putting the paper down and getting out of the recliner—let alone fighting off an intruder.

But, be that as it may, my nine-year-old boy, Samuel, was tired of losing his wrestling matches with me. He decided, therefore, to draft Joe, an old college friend of mine whose family was visiting, to jump me as I was passing through the living room to the lunch table.

Unsuspectingly, I walked into their trap (of course, I was thinking about food) and Joe quickly got me into a half Nelson wrestling hold. Despite my pleas of "Ah . . . Ah . . . Joe. That's my neck you have there," Joe refused to let go. I felt totally at his mercy. As a slender office-bound lawyer for years I was bewildered where he got the muscles. Suddenly, Samuel changed sides and started pulling Joe off me, which gave me just what I needed to break out of Joe's vice grip.

Later, Samuel explained how shocked he was in seeing me, his dad, actually losing (in his mind he probably figured I could take on five Joes with one arm tied behind my back). But it took only seconds, he said, before he knew he had to save me. His face beamed at the thought of rescuing his dad.

I knew his view of me as *"Dad the Invincible"* would come to an end eventually and I was glad it wasn't too dramatic a revelation for him. This was confirmed the other day when he asked me to take out his stuck trumpet mouthpiece for him. I said, "No problem" but ducked into the hallway just to avoid possible embarrassment in front of our dinner guests.

Unfortunately, despite my facial grimaces and color changes, the part remained frozen.

Samuel then looked at me like we shared a guarded secret and with a twinkle in his eye said, "Should I ask Mr. Besson to get it out for me?"

I said, "No" and he took the trumpet as it was to his music lesson. Later, he said in a serious tone, "You know, Dad, there was a guy half your age at school who took out that mouthpiece." He waited for dramatic effect before he smiled and added, "But he used oil."

"God opposes the proud but gives grace to the humble."
(1 Peter 5:8)

Other verses to look up: **1 Corinthians 12**

Questions:

When it comes to pride, what tendency do you have—to think you are superior to others or inferior? Why are both wrong according to the Word of God?

What gifts of the spirit do you think you possess and why?

What do the other members of the family think are your special gifts?

The Challenges of Hanging On to an Old Car

I should have known that once I voiced out loud that I wanted to keep my 1988 car another year things would happen to test my resolve. The decision was a no-brainer based on the fact we had no money after just buying a house. The car had only cost $2,000 and it still ran two years later. What was one more year?

I had even adjusted to the car's little idiosyncrasies like the bucking Bronco routine between gears, especially after rainstorms, and drinking too much oil. I had also learned to ignore the little things that needed fixing like the material hanging from the driver's door, the blinkers that blinked too fast, the rubber lining around the trunk opening that became unglued, and the cassette player that only played when you pressed on it with your fingers (little tough to do when you have a stick shift).

What I wasn't prepared for was the muffler pipe getting bent by scraping against the iron piece in the middle of our new driveway, which is there so we can close the metal gate. The noise the car now makes acts as a public service announcement to the community that we are within 50 miles.

I also wasn't prepared for my wife driving into the gate because she was trying to avoid hitting the iron thing in the driveway. The fender dent was significant and she also broke part of the thin chrome piece on the bumper, which then kept popping out of its groove at regular intervals. I had to remember to keep pushing it back into place or it could double as a lance that could run through somebody that got too close.

This problem was solved when my 12-year-old daughter, Alicia, got out of the car to open the gate and ran into it. Being a good dad I quickly jumped out of the car and ripped the culprit from its place and threw it in the garbage can while my wife consoled her. Fortunately, she hadn't taken a direct hit.

I was also unprepared for what happened a few days later. I had borrowed a little trailer to take the yard debris to the dump. I set it by the garage to use later.

Meanwhile, my wife was getting overwhelmed with the kids' high energy and decided to channel it toward constructive action. She saw the trailer and the messed up yard and said, "All right, children. Why don't you clean up the yard?"

In her zeal, my daughter picked up the front of the trailer with her two brothers, six and nine, and managed to turn it around. Unfortunately, she also discovered too late that the trailer was heavy. It rolled into the driver's side fender.

When I was told of the accident Alicia said adamantly that the dent was already there. I investigated the damage and the trailer must either have caused it, or, they were playing catch with a bowling ball and somebody missed. I did not feel angry but felt I must conduct a reality check with Alicia: "That, my girl, (pointing to the affected area) was not there previously." She responded with a non-committal, "Humph."

These events remind me of a Bible verse in James 1:2-3 that says, *"Consider it pure joy, my brothers, whenever you face trials of many kinds, because you know that the testing of your faith develops perseverance."*

I can't say that I've arrived at "pure joy" status yet in regards to these car trials ("detached joy" maybe) but I'm working on it.

I'll keep you posted if the dent collector and I make it through the year together.

Other verses to look up: **1 Peter 1:6 & 7**

Questions:

Why is it hard to rejoice during trying times?

Is there something you can do to help keep a good attitude during these periods?

Is there something that God may being trying to teach you through this difficulty?

Is there anyone going through some trials right now at school or at work?

Pray for one another.

Insects

Some people struggle over big theological issues like Calvinism or Arminianism; if the rapture will occur before or after the tribulation; if the spiritual gifts are for today or not; or if young people sporting tongue ornaments should be allowed on the worship team (if only to prevent accidental electrocutions).

I struggle with more practical questions during summer months such as: Why did God create insects? I know part of my problem comes from poor grades in science but, still, are they really that necessary to the ecological balance of nature? All right. We can keep the bees for the honey, butterflies because they look nice, the Bombardier Beetle to confuse evolutionists, the Praying Mantis because he reminds us to pray, but as far as I am concerned, the other uglies can go—mosquitoes, gnats, ticks, spiders, wasps, cockroaches, yellow jackets, fleas, locusts, flies, etc.

I guess what exacerbates this problem for me is the fact the French do not believe in window screens for some reason.

Flies and other flying arthropods are, therefore, constantly invading my living space without my permission. So what do I do? Buy an ugly brown fly strip and destroy the aesthetics of our home and risk getting my hair stuck in it as I walk by (I still have delusions that I have hair)? Or, just learn to co-exist peacefully with them?

This question hit me full force last Sunday afternoon as I was trying to take a nap on our living room sofa. I immediately heard the irritating buzz of an enemy fly and noticed him (or her) zigzagging in a two-foot square block of air space near our living room ceiling light (it wasn't on) for about five minutes. I was content that he wasn't being obnoxious by hop-scotching across my face but I wondered why he was doing what he was doing. What sense did all his frantic activity really add to the grand symphony of life? It was almost like he was saying: "C'mon, Big Fella. Get up and try and hit me if you can!" It also led me to thinking about heights and if there was a certain altitude where insects would not go. I wondered, too, if they received lessons from their parents on how to really annoy humans. It would probably go something like this:

"The first thing you do is land on the tip of his nose. Stay for two seconds and then fly away. Return in three seconds but this time land on the bald spot in the middle of his head. If he is eating make sure you land on the ravioli on his fork just before he puts it in his mouth. Do not be alarmed when he drops everything to chase you around the apartment swinging a dishtowel. If you are lucky he will break lamps, dispute with his wife about doing such things while at the dinner table, and fall over a toy on the floor. This kind of ridiculous

behavior makes it all worthwhile. Beware of a moustached man on the 3rd floor of Le Resseguin. He will stop at nothing to exterminate us from the face of the earth! Anything you can do to make his life miserable can qualify you for a dumpster vacation at a meat packing plant in Kansas!"

There seems to be absolutely no reason Noah should have brought two mosquitoes onto the ark. Then I met an insect lover from England named Colin Figures. After sharing my questions and some animated discussions, we agreed on at least one point—the nasty type insects that do harm to humans probably became so after the fall similar to the animals that became carnivorous.

When I mentioned my irritation with flies he said, with a twinkle in his eye, "Just think of how amazing it is that such little creatures can make such turns and take-offs! Engineers still can't invent something that small that can do that!"

After I pressured him to explain if all insects were really necessary in making the world go 'round, he said, "All creatures were made to give glory to Him in one way or another. It doesn't really matter if they are utilitarian. They were birthed out of the creative generosity of God!"

I always enjoy discussing a subject with someone who is passionate about it. But if you will excuse me, I have a date with a fly at the O.K. Corral.

God blessed them and said to them,
"Be fruitful and increase in number; fill the earth and subdue it.
Rule over the fish of the sea and the birds of the air and over every
living creature that moves on the ground."
(Genesis 1:28)

Questions:

What is Calvinism and Arminianism?

Is there something in the Bible or in your experience that you don't understand?

Do a study in the Bible on this subject and then present your findings to the family next week.

The Story of Old Simon

Most people have heard the story about the man who had a dream of walking on a beach. In the dream the man sees two sets of footsteps in the sand representing Jesus walking with him throughout his life. During the worst trials of his life, however, he noticed there was only one set of footsteps. Appalled that God would abandon him at such times he complained, "Lord, you promised when I gave my life to you that you would never leave me nor forsake me and yet during the most troublesome moments of my life there are only one set of footprints." God's response brings the truth home in astounding simplicity and no doubt humbled the man greatly: "My precious child, I love you and I would never leave you. During your times of trial and suffering, when you see only one set of footprints in the sand, it was then that I carried you."

God promises us in His word, the Bible: *"Come near to God and he will come near to you"* (James 4:8). Sadly, there are times when we just don't believe it.

A story with a similar theme has been circulating in Europe since the 1930s about an old man named Simon. According to oral tradition, a sexton of an ancient Protestant church observed something odd going on in the building for which he was responsible. Every day at precisely 12 noon an old man would enter the sanctuary of the church, stay for about five minutes, and then leave.

Since the sexton was in charge of the church's maintenance and to safeguard its contents, he was naturally concerned what this man was doing in there. He didn't see anything missing or damaged after the man's visits so he couldn't figure out what lay behind the man's actions.

Finally, curiosity getting the best of him, the sexton approached the man as he was leaving the church and asked him point blank, "Excuse me, sir, but I've seen you come into the church for the last several months at 12 p.m. every day, stay only for five minutes, and then leave. What exactly do you do in there?"

At first, the man seemed taken aback that someone had actually been observing him for so long but then he gave this reply: "Oh, I just go up to the altar and say, 'Lord, I don't know how to pray but my name is Simon and I just wanted you to know that I was here.'"

Satisfied that the peculiar man had told the truth, the sexton didn't bother him again. One day, however, the strange ritual stopped and the sexton didn't see the old man again. Word got back to him that old Simon had been in a serious accident and was at the hospital.

Meanwhile, at the medical facility, despite his grave physical condition, old Simon was radiant with joy and lifting the spirits of everybody there, including the entire hospital staff. When they asked him why he was so happy he said it was because of a regular visitor who came to see him.

This response, of course, mystified everyone even further because there was no record of anyone ever having come to see him since his admission into the hospital. It was also well-known that old Simon had no family or friends in the area.

After much coaxing, old Simon explained: "Every day at exactly 12 noon a man comes to the foot of my bed and he says, 'Hello, Simon, my name is Jesus and I just wanted you to know that I was here' and then he leaves."

"Come near to God, and he will come near to you."
(James 4:8)

Other verses to look up: **Hebrews 13:5, John 14:18**

Questions:

Can you think of any Bible characters who may have felt that God had abandoned them?

Have you ever felt abandoned by God or that He doesn't hear your prayers? When do you usually think this way?

Is this sense of abandonment based on a feeling or a fact?

What can you do when you feel alone and misunderstood?

Did God have a greater purpose for the Bible characters? What was it for the ones that you mentioned? Had God really abandoned them?

Signs of Getting Older

Aging happens. As someone approaching the half-century mark, I should know. A distinction should be made, however, between "getting older" and "being old." Old is always 15 years beyond where you are. It is also what people usually say about other people. My Mom, at 83, would say she is a mature senior citizen. Her Mom, who just turned 103, is old. Yet "getting older" is what we do every second of every day.

I remember clearly when I was 34 and I met a white-haired ruddy looking fellow who confessed he was 50. I didn't voice it out loud but my thoughts at the time were something like this: *Wow. This dude is old! With a little polish he could probably check into a museum.*

Now, I see people who are 75 or 80 as old. (Please don't tell my Mom.) It still remains a mystery to me, though, why we come into the world looking like a chubby-cheeked Winston Churchill and go out resembling a rooster with a flabby double chin. As a Christian it can be a wonderful time to grow in humility and discover how much stock you put into your "looks." The

Apostle Paul had it right when he said in 2 Corinthians 4:16: *"Therefore we do not lose heart. Though outwardly we are wasting away, yet inwardly we are being renewed day by day."* He knew the truly important thing in life was not how he appeared on the outside but how he looked to God on the inside.

We can be in denial, however, about this whole process of "wasting away." The following are just a few telltale signs that can help us come face to face with our mortality:

1.) When you show your friends your photo from the high school yearbook and they all look at you and the photo and then laugh and say spontaneously in perfect harmony, "Nawwwww!"

2.) When you lose at tennis to a 10-year-old boy and you justify your loss by saying he had a better racket or he plays just like Pete Sampras did as a boy. Of course, you have no idea how P.S. played as a boy but you have fallen into deep delusion to preserve the little athletic self-esteem you may have left.

3.) When your conversation with your doctor goes something like this when he tries to scoot you out of his office with an over-the-counter drug and send you a $50 bill for five minutes work: "Hey, Doc, wait a minute! I got his lump here on my arm I thought you should look at . . . and my back has been bothering me a little lately . . . and let's not forget, I've had a little reflux lately . . . and . . . and . . ." It's not that you are psychosomatic; you just want to get your full money's worth for the visit.

4.) When you have a slight pain in the chest area and you call the family together for a final farewell speech—only to discover it was only a chest muscle reacting to the marble table you tried to move yesterday.

5.) When a young hairdresser stops for a moment of quiet meditation as she gets to the rear aerial view of your head because she is embarrassed to tell you about the discount for balding men.

6.) When your Mom, after decades of getting you the correct underwear for Christmas, suddenly grossly exaggerates your girth and buys you something that would fit a member of the World Wrestling Association.

7.) When you look in the mirror in the morning and automatically say, "Dad?"

So, if you feel old right now, relax. You've got another 15 years. Maybe.

"Therefore we do not lose heart. Though outwardly we are wasting away, yet inwardly we are being renewed day by day."
(2 Corinthians 4:16)

Other verses to look up: **1 Kings 12:1-19, Proverbs 20:18**

Questions:

Do you have a negative attitude against older people? If so, why?

What may be an advantage of listening to an older person when seeking advise as opposed to a younger person?

Why do you think Rehoboam followed the advice of his friends rather than the elders?

Whose advice carries more authority in your life? (Perhaps a question to reflect upon in silence).

Baseball, Freshly Cut Grass, and Good Team Ethics

I can't help it, but every time I cut the lawn, I smile. The reason is simple. I smell the wonderful odors of the grass and a wave of pleasant memories come flooding back about my favorite childhood pastime—playing baseball.

Hardball was reserved for the official baseball leagues, with my dad as coach, while neighborhood games meant softball every day, if it didn't rain. All we needed was a tee shirt, a cap, a ball, gloves, and we were all set.

Mom excelled in the cookie department and gave a shout whenever her newest variety came out of the oven and needed consumption. Of course, they were quickly washed down with milk or juice in short order and then it was back to the business at hand.

When the official baseball season arrived, a freshly mowed field meant "real" games with nine kids on the team, uniforms, and ice cream cones at the local Dairy Queen, whether we won or lost. Although dad liked to win as much as all of us, he didn't feel it was the only thing. If you played your best, regardless of the outcome, you deserved a reward.

There was camaraderie, too, and we all rooted for each other. We all had a goal to win and we knew we needed each other to accomplish that end. Ritchie Griffiths was our long ball slugger, Gary Portal our catcher, Gary Watkins our third baseman, and Stu Pratt our southpaw pitcher.

I still remember shivering in my sneakers the first time my dad put me up to bat against the ferocious fast ball pitcher, Ritchie Muskarella. I was just a pipsqueak my first year and my dad figured I might be able to get on base with a walk. Despite my dad's best advice of: "Don't swing! Just stand there and make him pitch!" I struck out anyhow.

Eventually, with a lot of guidance and perseverance, I became a decent shortstop with a good batting average.

My dad also believed strongly in keeping players alert and maintaining a high morale by constant "pepper" or encouragements from the team. If it got too quiet out on the field he would yell, "I don't hear any chatter out there," and we would burst into a spontaneous chorus like overzealous crickets: "C'mon, Stu, burn it by 'em. Burn it by 'em" or "Two out! Two outs! Only one more. We can do it." Of course, my dad would draw the line against derogatory personal comments about the opposing players or off-color jokes.

When I think about it, some of those ingredients that helped us do well as a team could also be applied to almost any group, whether it be a company or a church.

1.) Understand that you need each other if you are going to succeed *(1 Corinthians 12)*.
2.) Do the best you can and it is a reward in itself *(Colossians 3:23)*.

3.) Speak positively to one another frequently
(Hebrews 3:13).
4.) Don't speak harshly of other people or groups
(2 Timothy 2:24).

If all the members of our groups or churches practiced these principles it would surely be a sweet aroma to outsiders and might even interest people in joining us, or listening to what we have to offer.

Ah . . . there's nothing like freshly cut grass!

Questions:

How would you rate your team (family) in the following four categories?
* *Understanding your need for each other.*
* *Doing your best at your job or chore no matter what it is.*
* *Encouraging one another frequently.*
* *Not speaking badly of other teams or families.*

What are your strong points?

Where would you say you need improvement?

Ten Ways to Overcome the Fear of Flying

My six-year-old son and I struggle with a fear of flying. On a recent flight to France I wondered if he was going to be as hysterical as he was the previous time. When we talked about it beforehand Sammy seemed excited, so I thought maybe he had lost his fear. I changed my mind, though, after the stewardess explained what to do in case of an emergency. When the oxygen mask came down, and she put it over her mouth, Sammy took an unhealthy interest in the emergency chart in the seat pocket in front of him. He kept pulling it out and coming back to the same questions: "Dad. What is the plane in the picture doing in the water?" and "Dad. What will happen to us if the plane goes in the ocean?" I thought honesty was the best policy so I responded, "Son. We will die and go see Jesus."

Meanwhile I also kept trying distracting tactics like pointing with one hand out the window and saying, "Hey Samster, we're going through the clouds now! Isn't that neat!" and grabbing hold of his emergency chart with my other hand

and forcing it in the pocket for him. Overall Sammy did great and enjoyed the flight enormously—especially when he fell asleep on my lap for five hours. (I am now convinced that heads are the heaviest parts of our bodies.) Of course that made it a little difficult for me to nod off, so I had my struggles. The following are the five dos and don'ts for people who are quietly or dramatically fearful of riding 30,000 feet above the ground going 400 miles an hour with a pilot whose license they have never seen.

Don'ts

1.) Don't try to analyze why planes don't carry parachutes.

2.) Don't try to figure out, while you are looking at the pretty specks of lights of the cities below, if the plane broke apart and you were thrown out of the plane, if you would die in the air from a lack of oxygen on the way down, or you would have a great sky-diving experience and then have a rather abrupt stoppage.

3.) Don't try to put yourself in a fetal position underneath your neighbor's seat. You won't fit.

4.) Don't think about the old criticism of air travel: If God wanted us to fly He would have given us wings.

5.) Don't wonder why scientists spend so much time with microchips and computers and don't think of ways to make a parachute smaller so you can wear it on your back during a flight. (Forget it. People afraid of flying would just think it was like a placebo and wasn't real, or if it was real, theirs would be the only one to malfunction in time of a crisis.)

Dos

1.) Think about how your fear doesn't change anything. If your plane goes down it will go down if you are afraid or not. You might as well enjoy the ride. If the plane hits some turbulence just pretend you are on a roller coaster and yell "Geronimo!" as loud as you can.

2.) If you are with your family at least you will all go together and not have to worry about what to get them for Christmas next year.

3.) Think about how statistically it is more dangerous to ride in a car than in an airplane. (Didn't work for me: I totalled a car a month before take-off).

4.) Pray and meditate on the Bible verse from 2 Timothy 1:7, which states: *"For God did not give us a spirit of timidity, but a spirit of power, of love and of self-discipline."*

5.) Think about how great Christians such as David Wilkerson from *Cross and the Switchblade* fame are afraid of flying. At least that is what I heard somewhere. (Anyone knowing if this is true or not please let me know with a signed letter—with the Times Square Church letterhead—from Mr. W.)

On a more serious note: psychiatrists tell us that most of the things we fear will never take place. Statistically, being in a plane crash in a jet across the Atlantic is rather remote. The fear of dying, however, is based on fact. We will all die at one time or another despite how many miles we run a week, vitamins we take, granola bars we eat, or the number of security systems we have in our homes. When I told Sammy we would go see Jesus if the plane crashed, his immediate concern was for the other people in the plane: "But Daddy, do all these people know Jesus?" For most of us, it is very unlikely that our *planes* will crash, but one thing is certain—one day all our *plans* will.

Our eternity will rest on how we answer Sammy's question.

*"Just as man is destined to die once, and after that to face judgment,
so Christ was sacrificed once to take away the sins of many people;
and he will appear a second time, not to bear sin, but to bring
salvation to those who are waiting for him."*
(Hebrews 9:27 & 28)

Other verses to look up: **Philippians 4:6, 2 Timothy 4:2**

Questions:

Are you afraid of anything right now in your life?

*Take some time to share your anxieties and pray together using the
verse from Philippians as a guide.*

*Are there people in your life right now who you see regularly but
have never prayed for, or with whom you have never shared the
good news of Jesus Christ?*

*Share the names and pray together that God will touch their lives
and that you will have opportunities to share with them this week.*

Shopping For a Purse

Shopping for me is like a hunt. Track it down, kill it, bag it, and take it home. Wandering aimlessly from one aisle to another under fluorescent lights is not my idea of a good time. My motto when it comes to shopping is: *Tell me what you want and I will get it for you.* All right, it might not be the exact thing you want but at least it will be in the same family, generally speaking of course.

Having said all that, I want you to know that I do occasionally make the ultimate sacrifice and "go shopping" to buy a gift for my wife. My first experience of this nature was shortly after our wedding. She needed a purse (I prided myself on the fact that I saw this need without being told) and I was going to buy one for her. Unfortunately, I went with an unmarried friend and we were a classic case of "the blind leading the blind." Together we chose what we thought was a perfectly functional brown leather purse.

When my wife opened the package her face did not register the joy I had anticipated. Yes it was a nice thought, she said, but totally lacking in aesthetic qualities and something she would not be caught dead toting around town. I tried to convince her of its beauty by hanging it up and changing its position daily in our hotel room so she could see it from every angle, but she refused to budge. Reluctantly, I let her bring the purse back.

Over the years, the sting of that first shopping "faux pas" lifted and I eventually enjoyed some successes in buying gifts for my wife. Then, not too long ago, my wife said, "I need a new purse" and the memory of that first excursion reappeared in living color (brown). Having matured since then, however, I had the boldness to say, "Great. Let's go buy one."

What surprised me was my willingness to go with her on what could prove to be a long and tedious expedition. I told her I would go but only as an observer.

As a result, I learned much about the marketing of women's purses. For example, some companies believe that the endorsement of a famous actress will seduce her fans to buy the purse. Others believe a lot of pockets or custom-made slots for cell phones, calculators, or credit cards will win the career ladies over. And, just to make sure nobody is left out, purses come in every conceivable variety of sizes, colors, and designs—large purses, small purses, purses with buckles, purses with zippers, purses with funny graphics, plastic purses, leather purses, blow up purses, and strap-on-your-back purses. I marvelled at the creativity of man to come up with so many different forms for the basic purse.

I was also intrigued by Véronique's selective process. Methodically, she went to several bins and checked them out. If she found an interesting purse, she would put the strap over her shoulder and then look in a mirror to see if the purse was a match. She then chatted with the purse lady to learn if there were any special sales. She wasn't impulsive or overtly attached to any of the cowhides or synthetic materials. She remained emotionally aloof and displayed a business-like acumen similar to a woman at a fish market who knew her business and would not be hoodwinked.

Finally, she decided on a reasonably-priced black leather purse with gold-colored snaps. I told her it looked mighty fine with her red winter coat and gladly wrote out a check for $20 less than what I would have paid.

Before leaving, I also took note that all of the obviously unpopular purses that filled the 50% off bin were brown and totally lacking in creative originality. I chuckled and said to myself—*must be a guy who designed that one!*

> *"Husbands, in the same way be considerate as you live with*
> *your wives, and treat them with respect as the weaker partner*
> *and as heirs with you of the gracious gift of life,*
> *so that nothing will hinder your prayers."*
> **(1 Peter 3:7)**

Another verse to look up: **Philippians 4:12**

Questions:

Have you noticed how advertisers are always trying to manipulate you to buy their product?

Watch a TV commercial together or pull out a magazine ad and talk about how the advertising company is trying to snag you.

Have you ever been reeled in by an ad and then later regretted buying the product?

Don't Go Gently into that Good Night

"**A**ccording to the car map here, Russell, it should be the next house," Patricia Nabor said to her husband as she stared at the small computer screen on the dashboard and then quickly looked out the window.

"That's it!" she cried. "There!"

He slowed the new 2008 dark blue Toyota Spirit-Master to a crawl and he also saw the white numbers on the wooden red mailbox that looked like an old covered bridge from another era in Vermont's history. He turned the car right and heard the squishing of mud from the tires and hoped he could limit the brown specks on the car. He didn't have time for a car wash today and he wanted to look as professional as possible for Mr. Winston Cowley, who had money to burn on his company's high-risk mutual funds. The sunny early April morning was already melting the snowfall from last week and the fields they passed on both sides of the long curving drive-way had clusters of white amidst the brownish green grass. They passed a row of pine trees and the magnificent Victorian mansion came into view, complete with a wrap-around porch. It looked just like it did in the literature—a beautifully restored early 19th century home.

For many years it had served as a private museum because a well-known writer had lived there, but due to the fact most schools had dropped his books from the required reading lists, the tourist trade also suffered. Consequently, it was sold to the highest bidder. The winner happened to be a medical association specializing in expirations.

Patricia flipped down the mirror located on the reverse side of the sun visor and turned up her face to check her make-up. Since she had recently become a national director of a cosmetic company, she was even more attentive to her own looks which she considered her best advertising. She also prepared a free sample basket of products for the counselor they were seeing. Who knows, she thought, maybe his wife or girlfriend had a birthday coming up. She often picked up regular customers by being so bold.

Russell parked the car near the front door and then spoke a telephone number into the air. Immediately the sound of dialing erupted from four speakers and then ringing. The phone rang three times before a man's voice answered.

"Hello, Nabor Insurance and Investments, can I help you?"

"Peter," Russell began authoritatively, "just want you to know I'll be a little late to the office this morning. Please call back the guy who called yesterday about life insurance. Set up an appointment if you can for this week. Also, please get Diane going on the investments series. You know the one that covers mutual funds, annuities, and whole life. I think everybody else has some things to work on. Any problems, just send me a message on my E-Band."

"No problem Mr. Russell. Anything else?"

"That's it for now, Pete. I'll see you later."

Russell said, "Off," and the sound from the speakers ceased. He turned to his wife and said, "Well, you ready, beautiful?" He liked her new French style haircut with her dark auburn hair curling around her ears and touching her neck just above her shoulders. He wasn't surprised she was promoted to the national director position and on track for the silver Porsche. She was a real go-getter and didn't let much get in her way. The competing company only offered Cadillacs. As a result, she was able to recruit some of their best sales people who needed a bigger carrot dangling to keep them motivated. His only complaint was when she ran out of the house for an appointment and left him to take care of their 10- and 8-year-old boys without advance notice. But he could put up with that, now and then, to drive her Porsche.

"Ready when you are," she said, popping her cosmetics brush into her bag, clipping it closed, and placing it in the glove compartment. "We've got exactly four minutes before our appointment with the psychologist Stephen Coobs." After getting out of the car, Russell turned to the car door and pointed his key case like it was a 45. Automatically all the doors locked with a clinking sound. His wife smiled and said, "Really, Russell. Do you really think you need to lock it here out in the country?"

"Just a habit from working in Albany so much. You never know. Thieves are everywhere. You don't want anyone to lift your eyebrow plucker do you?"

"Very funny," Patricia responded. "You men just don't understand how much time it takes to look beautiful for you." With a dramatic flair she tossed her white and red silk scarf just above the collar of her long red cashmere winter coat. Her mood changed, though, as they walked up the stone-paved walkway. She squinted her eyes in a serious expression and looked directly at her husband.

"Russell. Are you sure you want to go through with this?"

He returned her look and said, "Absolutely." Then he turned away.

Their shoes made loud dull hollow sounds from the gray wooden porch as they approached the front door. A robin sang in the distance; the air just a touch chilly for the time of year. Russell quickly read the carved wooden sign attached to the door, *Please don't knock, just come in,* and pushed their way in. He took Patricia's overcoat and hung it on the coat rack and then took off his own Pierre Carden black wool overcoat and hung it next to hers. He then turned his neck slightly in both directions as if he needed to buy some room in a space limited by his stiff white collar and perfectly tied red cravat. His black suit was Italian and so were his black shoes. He was about six feet, 220 pounds and in good shape from daily running and weekly visits to the tennis club. The creeping double chin bugged him, though. A friend had ribbed him once that he should have it surgically removed and then made into a wallet—an idea he didn't find too amusing. Afterward, he had subconsciously started a frog-like ritual of sucking it up whenever he looked into the mirror.

"It's the first door on the right," Patricia commented. She now felt a little odd carrying her basket of samples, like she was little red riding hood going to grandmother's house, but a phrase immediately came to mind which she often said to her sales group, *Don't let your little anxieties stand in the way of your success,* and she straightened up in a confident position. Suddenly, a thought came into her head that scared her. What if he's a homosexual? Her professional mind kicked into gear: *Suggest that he give it to his wife, or, his mother.* Perfect, she thought. She was ready.

The hall was carpeted and Grandma Moses paintings hung from the walls. They approached the room and found the door was open. They could see books of psychology with names like Skinner, Perls, and Jung on the spines lining the wall straight ahead including a slim volume with the title, *The Psychology of Expirational Medicine.* They had to enter and go left to meet its occupant. Before entering, however, Russell knocked on the door lightly and called, "Hello? Anybody home?" Immediately a friendly nasal sounding voice said, "Please come in Mr. and Mrs. Nabor. I was expecting you." As they rounded the corner, a thin curly blond-haired man of about 35 jumped up from behind a large mahogany desk and stretched forth his hand in greeting. He shook Russell's hand firmly and said, "Steve Coobs. Glad to meet you both." He then shook Patricia's hand with a slightly softer touch and motioned for them to sit down in the matching brown leather chairs behind them. With a wide smile, he sat in a similar chair directly across from them.

"Glad you could come together. I know you are both incredibly busy. Any trouble finding the place?"

"No. Not at all. Our car map does all the work. It's just a little different from the other expiration centers we've visited."

"Well, I think we have a different philosophy than most of them. Personally, I don't think some health groups are very sensitive to people. They build a sterile clinic-like center instead of making people feel at home. I think the best place for an expiration is at home with the family. But, as you know, that legislation hasn't passed yet, so we just have to do the next best thing and have them here. Government controlled, you know. I guess it is a little easier keeping track when there are centers."

"You mean there are expirations going on right now as we speak?" Patricia asked incredulously, bending her left hand at the wrist and pointing in the direction of where they had just come in.

"Oh no, Mrs. Nabor. We never plan an expiration on the same day as an interview. We believe that is a very private time for a family and we don't allow anyone on the property except only authorized personnel and family members."

Patricia leaned back into the brown leather chair, apparently relieved by the response.

"In fact," Coobs continued, "we can provide an empty room if the family wants to bring personal items from the house and recreate the home atmosphere, at no extra expense, of course."

Russell thought it strange that he would mention that an empty room would be "at no extra expense." Why would anyone pay extra for an empty room? He immediately dismissed it as irrelevant to their visit.

"That's great," said Russell, affirming the positive in his mind. "It must be comforting to have familiar things in the room with you when you expire. By the way, Mr. Coobs, how many expirations do you do a year?"

"We're not a factory here, Mr. Nabor, and we are not profit-making as some of our competitors are. Our priorities are to do what's best for our clients, making sure they know exactly what they are doing, providing painless expirations, and post expiration counselling for family members, if needed."

"What do you mean by post expirational counselling, Mr. Coobs?" Patricia asked, turning her head slightly with a puzzled look on her face and twisting the end of her hair nervously. She stopped abruptly when she caught herself doing it. Teenage habits die hard, she thought.

"Well, sometimes, Mrs. Nabor, family members have to deal with what we call "false guilt." It doesn't happen too much these days, with all the expirations taking place but we probably get two or three a year."

There was a long silence. Then Patricia spoke:

"Well, honey, are you going to tell him, or what?"

"Yes. Of course. I was going to get around to it eventually," he said, a little more gruffly than he intended.

Steven Coobs leaned forward in his chair toward the couple with intensely concerned eyes and asked gently, "Tell me what, Mr. Nabor? Are you having any problems with the potential expiree, by any chance?"

"Well, now that you mention it, my father doesn't seem too keen on the idea. We've tried the best arguments provided by your foundation, like: he won't suffer as much, the grandkids won't have to experience the trauma of seeing him suffer, and he won't have to die in isolation and loneliness in a nursing home somewhere . . ."

"Those will be obsolete, or should I say, unnecessary in 10 years. No question," Coobs interjected decisively with a wave of his hand. "But please, Mr. Nabor, tell me exactly: what is your father dying of?"

"AIDS, Mr. Coobs. Not full-blown AIDS yet, but he has been diagnosed with HIV positive since the blood transfusion he had during his heart operation. I've tried to tell him of the horrible death that is awaiting him but he still refuses to expire. I've even shown him pictures of people with AIDS just before they died. He still won't see the wisdom in it."

"I'm surprised he got it that way these days. Hospitals are usually pretty diligent about the blood filtering. Tough break for him, though. I understand, Mr. Nabor. Can I ask you something else?

They nodded in unison.

"Does he belong to a religious sect of any kind?"

"Why yes, Mr. Coobs," Patricia almost screeched. "How did you know?"

"Well, it is quite common for these types to resist modern medicinal practices and philosophy. They are old fashioned and really very self-centered people. They don't think of the inconvenience they would be to you—a very responsible professional couple approaching the zenith of their careers, self-actualizing to a degree they could not even imagine possible in their day. They don't think of the traumatic effect their sickness will have on their grandchildren. And lastly, they are not thinking about the next generation that will follow in their footsteps. The money used to keep them alive could be used for AIDS research to cure the AIDS virus. If he is a real fanatic he might even (barely stifles a chuckle) believe that his god can heal him."

Both Russell and Patricia looked at each other with knowing sheepish smiles.

"But there is something you may not have considered."

Russell cast a glance over to Patricia and asked, "And what is that?"

"In special cases like yours you can get an official injunction from the U.S. Expiration Committee making the expiration mandatory. In other words, you give them the evidence and if they agree with you that your father's expiration is in his best interests, that of his family and of the future generation he will have to go through it if he likes it or not."

"You mean, force him to die," Russell said with his eyes widening.

"That's not the term we would use here, Mr. Nabor—but yes, he would be obligated to go through with an expiration."

"Wow. I didn't realize that option existed," Russell ejaculated.

"Yes. Most people don't and we don't encourage it until it becomes a last resort. You are also obligated to sign a paper saying you will tell no one of this option for top security purposes. You could call it 'tough love.' In other words, you make people accept what is best morally for themselves, their families, and the rest of society." Coobs let that last phrase settle like a profound truth needing time to germinate.

Russell brought his hand to his chin in a thinking pose and pressed his lips together as if considering the weight of what was just said. Patricia shifted her weight in her chair and brushed her hand across her thigh to smooth an imaginary wrinkle on her skirt.

Russell looked at his E-Band Net Watch. The small number in the upper corner indicated he had five e-mails since their arrival. He said, "Excuse me Mr. Coobs. You've given us a lot to think about but we have to be going. Thank you for your time. We'll be in touch."

They all stood up and shook hands. Patricia suddenly thought of her basket. She picked it up from the hardwood floor and stretched it out to the counselor with a big smile.

"Here Mr. Coobs. I thought you may like to have some cosmetic samples . . ." (she glanced at his left hand, saw a ring, and continued) ". . . for your wife."

"That's very kind of you Mrs. Nabor. I'm sure she will appreciate it. You did include your business card in there, I trust?"

She said yes and he winked.

"Great. Goodbye. If there is anything we can do, please don't hesitate to ask."

"Thank you, Mr. Coobs," Russell said as he shook the man's hand.

Back in the car, Patricia didn't interrupt the silence until they had almost crossed the New York-Vermont line. Finally, she blurted out, "So, Russell, what do you think?"

"I don't know Pat. I don't know. It's one thing if he is in agreement with it—but to force him, I don't know."

"Think about it Russell. We don't have the time to be with him. He'll be miserable the last days of his life. We've got our careers to think of. And the children, Russell. Think of the children. Do you want them to remember him as an emaciated skeleton? Can't you see, dear, it's best for him and them? It really is."

"I said I don't know. Let's leave it for later, okay?" Color was rising in his face and Patricia decided to let it go, for now.

Later that afternoon Russell decided to stop by to see his dad. The door was locked and a note was attached to the doorknob. It read: *Sorry to take off on you like this, buddy, but it seemed the best for all involved. Your option to my situation is not acceptable to me. Everything has been taken care of with the house. The new owners will be moving in next week. Please don't try and find me. I will contact you when things are a little more settled.* In shock and unbelief Nabor leaned to the left of the stoop and looked into the living room. It was completely bare of any furniture. Evidently, his father had just flown the coop.

"In everything I did, I showed you that by this kind of
hard work we must help the weak, remembering the word the Lord
Jesus himself said: It is more blessed to give than to receive."
(Acts 20:35)

Other verses to look up: **1 Thessalonians 5:14, Exodus 20:12,**
2 Corinthians 1:3-7

Questions:

How did you feel hearing this story, when you realized what was really happening?

Do you think this type of thing could happen if euthanasia is legalized?

Why not kill people like we do dogs and cats?

Can suffering have a purpose in our lives?

Rock Star

I walked past a video store the other day and saw a poster advertising a film for rent—*Rock Star*. The picture featured a young man with a determined face, long hair, and a guitar slung over his shoulder like he was someone going somewhere. I had to chuckle at the caption underneath: *The wannabe who gotta be.* I remembered my own deluded adolescent dream, and that of probably thousands of others of my generation, "the wannabes who failed to be."

It all started my junior year of high school when my friend, Anthony, asked my twin brother and I to be part of his rock group. He already played guitar and he would teach me to play rhythm and Tom the bass.

After mastering the basics, our biggest problem was finding a place to really let our amplifiers crank. Just when we were sounding exactly like Jimi Hendrix, with the mandatory fuzz box distortion, Anthony's father, a carpenter by trade, would march down the stairs into the basement with his bib jean overalls and bulging biceps and tell us "Either turn it down or pack up and go home!" Then, horror of horrors, he would command us to play while he sung his favorite ballad, "Blue Moon," in operatic style—a clear waste of time and wattage—while we would roll our eyes in obvious contempt of his inferior musical taste.

Our first gig was at a wedding reception. We considered it a success since they actually paid us a whopping five dollars a piece. Of course that was after continual hounding of the lovebirds by Anthony for months afterwards, but we did get paid and that made us professionals.

Anthony wasn't satisfied, however, with our falsetto sounding voices and enlisted a high school dropout named Joe who had a more macho voice. His weakness, however, was lyric memorization and we just about strangled him for always messing up the Rolling Stones' classic "Satisfaction." *"Can't get no…!"* Finally, we decided to give him a try despite his amnesia.

Word spread like gangrene that we had a rock group and Vinny, an organizer of the Catholic Youth Organization dances, asked us to perform on a real stage for $100.

We were psyched, but on the night of the dance, disaster hit. Joe arrived reeking of alcohol after repeated admonitions to lay off the stuff. Later, any pretense of impending stardom quickly vanished when Vinny reluctantly gave us the check and said bluntly, "I thought you guys were supposed to be good."

Acutely perceiving an obvious lack of public acclaim, Anthony made the tough decision and cut Tom and I from the roster in favor of more gifted musicians.

My dream of celebrity status didn't die however; it merely changed gears. I took a stab at the folk scene and sang songs by Cat Stevens, James Taylor, and Bob Dylan in a few bars and coffee houses.

I eventually abandoned the hopeless quest for stardom to search for the truth, which I eventually found in a personal relationship with Jesus Christ.

Anthony, despite his exceptional skills as a guitarist, never made rock star status either. Sadly, he died an early death at 32 of a rare form of cancer.

I picked up the guitar again after my conversion and began learning to worship God in song. Today, I am frequently asked to lead worship during church services and small Christian gatherings. I am thankful that Anthony took the time to teach me guitar, and that Jesus gave me a significance I could never obtain as a "rock star." Nothing compares to the love, peace, and purpose I have as a child of God.

I also discovered that to be a "star" in God's eyes is a lot simpler than being a big talent. Philippians 2:14-16 says, *"Do everything without complaining or arguing, so that you may become blameless and pure, children of God without fault in a crooked and depraved generation, in which you shine like stars in the universe as you hold out the word of life . . ."*

In other words if you want to be "The Rock's Star": don't complain, don't argue, and share the good news of Jesus Christ.

If we all did that we would make quite a constellation, wouldn't we?

Other verses to look up: **1 Thessalonians 5:16-18, Ephesians 3:12**

(cont'd.)

Questions:

Do you believe you are accepted in Christ right now? Or, do you feel you must do something significant before you can accept who you are?

Are you being faithful in little things or are you waiting for your big chance to make it big and despising small opportunities to serve others?

What are your dreams and what practical steps can you make now to realize them?

On Becoming
a Public Speaker

"**H**ey! He looks like a manikin!" a voice yelled out from the back of the auditorium. On stage was a short skinny kid, with a deadpan expression, telling a gruesome story about a famous actress who literally lost her head in a car accident. Chuckles and laughter rippled across the rows of seats as the boy tried to continue. Although the speech was meant to be a sobering message on the dangers of drinking and driving, it had just the opposite effect. When he finally sat down the speech teacher's remarks—"they're all a bunch of jerks"—didn't really help. He just wanted to be accepted by his peers and he had failed miserably.

Unfortunately, the boy in the story was yours truly at 15. I was absolutely petrified of speaking in front of people. Although I didn't know it at the time, this phobia is widespread and some surveys reveal many people rate public speaking as #1 on their list of fears—even above the fear of dying or getting a terminal disease.

Little did my classmates know I had died a thousand

deaths before walking on stage. I had been scheduled to speak four days earlier but we had such a terrible snowstorm in New York in 1967, school kept being closed.

While others were out sledding or pummeling one another with snow balls, I was in front of the large mirror in our living room with my 3 x 5 cards dutifully going over my speech. The first day school was cancelled I was overjoyed to have more time to prepare. I just continued giving my monologue to my image in the mirror—forcing a smile and repeating the text. The second day I felt like a death row victim given a reprieve by a compassionate governor. The third day I was sick of my speech and noticed I was looking more like a corpse by the minute with a creeping terror circling my eyes. The fourth day I was a basket case and hoping the guards would come and carry me away so I could get it over with.

Another experience of public speaking came at 16. Despite my silent pleas of "not me not me" during a class debate, my government teacher turned to me and asked my opinion. I got a hearty round of laughs when I just pointed my thumbs to the students on each side of me and said, "I agree with them." To me it was totally irrelevant that they had just given conflicting views on the subject. The idea was to get the spotlight off me as fast as possible.

Later, in college, my fear of public speaking metastasized into what you might call a full-fledged "mind freeze." I remember distinctly being in front of my biology class, supposedly part of a sophisticated panel of some sort, and my mind having a complete white-out. Blowtorches couldn't have melted the arctic frost that had somehow found its way into my stream of consciousness.

Today, however, I love to speak in public. How did

this change occur? The big reason was after I asked Jesus Christ into my life at 22 and sought to live according to the principles of the Bible, I understood that I was loved by the most important person in the universe—God. Now, when I speak I am secure in who I am rather than trying to gain my audience's approval with my words. Since I am free from the need to please people, I can be myself. As the Bible confirms: *"The fear of man will prove to be a snare, but whoever trusts in the Lord is kept safe"* (Proverbs 29:25). I can also be confident that God will give me something of value for my listeners.

To prepare for a speech I spend time in prayer beforehand and I make an outline of the main points with illustrations from daily life, instead of memorizing every word. I've found when I speak from my heart I connect best with my listeners.

For me, nothing beats the feeling of the Holy Spirit using me to encourage and inspire others—not even the applause and accolades of man (or jerks).

> *"The fear of man will prove to be a snare,*
> *but whoever trusts in the Lord is kept safe."*
> **(Proverbs 29:25)**

Another verse to look up: **Genesis 4:10-12**

Questions:

Do you speak up when someone says something that you believe is wrong, or do you remain silent?

Do you defend others when they are being ridiculed and picked on, or do you do the same to be part of the crowd?

(cont'd.)

Do you care more about what people think or what God thinks about issues?

Will you defend God's viewpoint even if you are the only one who agrees with it?

Old Ethics with New Technology

For the sake of our society I sometimes feel called upon to address topics that are mysteriously not written or talked about—blind spots, if you will, left untreated by the popular press. At first glance it may seem rude to mention them at all but they warrant our attention because we may be sending messages that we do not intend.

Case in point. Cell phones. I strongly believe this product should come with a set of rules for proper etiquette. For example, is it morally right to continue working with a buzz saw when someone calls you up? I realize it is a temptation to just tuck it between your chin and shoulder but . . . try to empathize with the guy on the other end yelling his head off just to make himself heard. It gives the not-so-subtle message that the person calling is not important and, in fact, a down right nuisance. Although this may be true, the noble thing to do is just tell the person that you will call them later after you have cut down the tree.

General rule #1: *If the person has trouble hearing you* *because of the work you are doing, it is better to talk another time.*

It may be polite as well, if you cannot give your wholehearted attention, to simply let the person know. For example, "Do you mind if I clip my toe nails (teach the dog new tricks, vacuum the floor, eat a Big Mac, watch TV, play games on the computer, etc.) as we speak?" At least this gives the person an option if he or she does not want to compete for your already divided attention.

Of course, this rule does not apply to women talking to other women because we all know they can do 10 things at once without a problem.

The killer is when people actually bring their cell phones to a worship service. Do they really believe that there is someone more important to hear from than God? I understand medical and emergency workers are sometimes on call, but why not just wear a vibrating beeper? When it vibrates, you just go outside the church and then use your phone. This is much more discreet and not an annoyance to the rest of the congregation. It makes sense that the devil and his cohorts would want to use modern technology to disrupt the worship of God.

A cell-phone-friendly church should have baskets in which people can deposit their cell phones before they enter the sanctuary—kind of like outlaws from the Wild West handing over their six shooters before coming to the negotiating table. The ushers could also stick nametags on them and show these people to a special section in the back. When they feel the vibes they could just exit quietly.

General Rule #2: *Disconnect before going into a church service or invest in a vibrating beeper that will not be a distraction to others.*

Now, the thing no one wants to talk about. Is it right to use the bathroom while talking on a cell phone? Flushing, by the way, is a dead give away. Is it okay just because no one can see you, or are there things you should not do while on the phone? A good question to ask yourself as to whether something is appropriate to do on the phone, or not, might be: Would I be embarrassed if someone asked me, "Hey, what are you doing now anyway?"

    General rule #3: *Do not do anything while on the phone that would embarrass you if someone asked you what you were doing.*

Cell phones are a wonderful invention but let's remember giving people our full attention and truly listening to them is even better.

> *"My dear brothers, take note of this:*
> *Everyone should be quick to listen . . ."*
> **(James 1:19)**

Another verse to look up: **Philippians 2:3**

Questions:

When someone is talking are you really listening to them or just rehearsing in your mind what you want to say once they have finished speaking?

Take time to listen to each member of the family as they share about something they consider important that happened today.

How do you feel when someone else does all the talking?

Is there a time when it is appropriate to just let the person talk and a time when it is inappropriate?

Todd Beamer: My Kind of Hero

In a recent interview Lisa Beamer states that her husband, Todd, was just "an ordinary man." I appreciate her modesty and her desire to discourage people from idolizing Todd and making him an American icon. Yet, his simple words, "Let's roll," before leading the passenger revolt on Flight 93 that had been taken over by terrorists have inspired a nation. I think this is because his words summarize succinctly an attitude that many of us want in time of crisis.

I remember clearly being in my office in the south of France on September 11, 2001 when a colleague said, "There's a news report saying the Twin Towers in New York have been hit by terrorists!" Being a New Yorker for most of my life I felt particularly affected by this tragedy. In shock, I drove to the nearest TV located at a friend's house and watched the towers fall. Having a vivid imagination, I kept visualizing myself inside the plane knowing it was going to hit the tower. It made me feel powerless and helpless. Then, to see pictures of people actually jumping out of the buildings horrified me.

Then I read of Flight 93 and Todd's brave decision to stop the hijackers. Apparently he had heard what had happened in New York and Washington. It seems clear because when the Airfone operator asked him, "Is that what you really want to do?" he said, "It's what we have to do." Looking at the map in the special issue of *Time* magazine right after the attacks, their direction was obvious—Washington D.C. It's reasonable, therefore, to assume that Todd knew the plane's intended final destination and he was going to do everything in his power to thwart it. He was acutely aware, too, that he needed the Lord to help him. He asked the operator to pray the Lord's prayer with him and then quoted Psalm 23 which includes the verse: *"Even though I walk through the valley of the shadow of death, I will fear no evil, for you are with me."* Then he calmly said to his fellow mutineers, "Let's roll."

Psychologists tell us in time of crisis we can either "fight" or take "flight." I read also of the other guy who hid out in the bathroom and just reported on what was happening on his cell phone. I can't say I was inspired much by his actions. If I was in the plane, I'd like to believe I would have responded like Todd but I can't say for sure I would have. He felt fear but he didn't let it paralyze him. He thought clearly through the implications of what he was doing both for himself—"I don't think we are going to get out of this thing"—and for the people in Washington. He inspired others to join him and then he led the charge.

As much as I hate to admit it, there is a part of me like the pig in the *Charlotte's Web* video who whined, "But I don't wanna die! I don't wanna die!" when the other animals say he's headed for the butcher. Yet, Todd's righteous anger to stop the evil and his refusal to be passive about it gives me hope that I, too, can do what is right for others in a crisis, even if it means I may experience severe personal consequences as a result.

Yes, Todd was perhaps an ordinary man but, with the help of God, he did an extraordinary thing—he gave his life in order that others may live. That's my kind of hero.

"Greater love has no man than this,
that he lay down his life for the life of his friends."
(John 15:13)

Another verse to look up: **Hebrews 12:2**

Questions:

Do you think you could have done what Todd did? Why or why not?

As a Christian, do you think it is right to stop people by force if they are intent on hurting others? Give examples.

Is there such thing as a "just" war? In your opinion, what would constitute a just war?

The Delights and Dangers of Reading

wasn't aware of how much reading was a part of my life until the day my twin brother, Tom, dubbed me, "The Reader." I guess there had been a lull in our conversation at some point and I had rudely grabbed the nearest magazine or book to fill in the gaps. Or, perhaps, I was heading in the direction of the bathroom carrying something to read under my arm. Regardless of why he had suddenly nailed me with this label, his words and their ominous tone cut me to the quick. Was I, in fact, addicted to reading? Was this habit merely serving as a security blanket or did I just have a commendable thirst for knowledge—even to the point of reading medicine bottles in the can if nothing else was available?

My earliest recollection of loving to read goes back to the fifth grade. My mother kindly provided the funds to order as many as six books at a time whenever the Scholastic Book Services paper came out in class. I loved the smell of new books and especially the adventures of young boys in novels by Robb White. Often I would test my parents' patience by reading by flashlight under the covers well past Dad's shout of "Lights out!"

Later, in college, I expanded my reading diet to books by authors across the centuries and as diverse as Homer and Mark Twain.

Now one of my chief literary pleasures is reading memoirs: travel books to distant lands, autobiographies, true adventures, and personal essays. Probably what attracts me most to this genre is learning the details of other people's lives and their intimate thoughts and feelings. I can relate to what a character in the film, *Shadowlands,* said to his professor, C.S. Lewis: "We read to know that we are not alone." As I read true stories I feel I am treated like a close friend with whom the writers can trust their most guarded secrets. I feel honored to be their confidant and thrilled to experience many lives vicariously through their books.

If I don't watch out, however, this reading pastime could lead me to be more interested in the "exceptional" lives of people I will never meet rather than the ordinary people now in my life; not unlike people who take an unhealthy curiosity in the details of movie stars' lives while possibly ignoring the basic needs of those around them. It could also make me impatient with the normal two-way relationships that develop much more slowly and take sometimes years to mature and deepen.

The positive side of reading memoirs, however, is, it helps me to understand God's delight and desire to live inside each one of us and to share the intimate details of our personal stories. Happily, once He has taken residence in our hearts through repentance and faith, we can also interact with Him through prayer, something we can't do with the celebrities or other people we read about. (Just try to contact one of those famous authors and you'll see what I mean. I worked as an interviewer of writers for three years and the more successful they were the harder it was to speak with them!) In the Gospel of John chapter 14, verse 23, however, God's desire is clear: *"If anyone loves me, he will obey my teaching. My father will love him, and we will come to him and make our home with him."* This means we can actually be close to the most exciting person in the Universe—God—and He loves us so much He'd like to move into our lives permanently!

Today, I try to be more sensitive to people rather than their libraries and reading material, or the book I am reading at the moment. After all, each person I meet has a story worth hearing about, if I will only take the time to discover the key to unlock its treasure.

Another verse to look up: **Matthew 5:43-47**

Question:

When is the last time you took a few moments to speak with someone you usually don't talk to?

Family projects:

Make a commitment to do that this week and report back to the family what happened.

Invite someone (family can pray about who) to come over for dinner who will probably never invite you over.

Bullies

et's talk about bullies. In the small town where I grew up, just 70 miles north of the Big Apple, in New York, we had our fair share of them. Consequently, I became an expert in bully watching. Being small and skinny during my early teens, I seemed to attract them like flies. Bullies, I observed, are similar to mean dogs—once they sense that you are afraid of them, they try to bite you. My first encounter with "tough guys" occurred in the school lavatory during a Saturday night dance. When I made my entrance two boys were waiting. One of them was my age, though looking older with a shadow for a moustache, named John; the other one was Crazy Ralph. Ralph was built like a bulldozer, played fullback on the varsity football team, and was known to go berserk during brawls. I quickly learned he wasn't there for biological reasons, but as a tutor. Our conversation went something like this:

John: Gotta dime? (This may seem like a reasonable request today but back then it could buy two candy bars.)

Me: (about to put my hand in my pocket and say, "All

I got is a dollar. Do you have change?" when I caught myself and said) No.

John: (as I was trying to make a hasty retreat back to where the normal people congregated) Wanna go out back and go a few rounds?

Me: No thanks (as I quickened my pace toward the saloon-type swinging doors that preceded the big door that led to the hallway).

Ralph: Just smack 'im, John.

John: (now pushing me from behind through the swinging doors with my head jerking backwards in typical whiplash-type fashion) C'mon you chicken.

Me: (Exit. Stage left).

In my heart, I believed that I had done the right thing. If I had accepted John's invitation and he started losing by some freak of nature—like falling into an open sewer hole or something—Crazy Ralph would have killed me with one haymaker to the forehead. At least that's what I told my friends. Still, my walking away bothered me. As a result, John and his younger brother, Steve, would haunt me throughout high school.

For many years after graduation I used to get angry just thinking about all the abuse I tolerated. Much later, however, I found out that many of these bullies became victims of their own warped personalities. Some became drug addicts. Some ended up in prison. Some were involved in fatal car accidents. Some, thankfully, were saved. Looking back, I can see how many of these guys were just pawns in the hands of a greater evil and, unfortunately, were later caught in his web.

Today, as a Christian, I know the devil is the only bully

out there that I need to watch out for. The Bible says that he *"prowls around like a roaring lion looking for someone to devour"* (1 Peter 5:8). In high school, part of my problem was I didn't know who I was, and therefore, had no confidence to stand up for what was right. Today, I know that my identity is "in Christ" and my fighting strategy is simple—I submit to God and resist the devil. The Bible says that he *must* flee from me if I fulfill these two conditions (James 4:7).

Of course, the enemy and his cohorts aren't always behind our problems, but sometimes they are, so we need discernment. To give you an example, years ago I was having a lot of trouble with an elderly supervisor at work. She would constantly tell me to do something and then, in the middle of doing it, she would tell me to do something else. Then she would get mad at me for not finishing the first thing she gave me to do. Her confusing instructions were doing a number on my mind and I was beginning to think I was a prime candidate for Looney Tunes. I mentioned my problem with a brother in the Lord and he said, "Let's do some spiritual warfare." We then took our positions in Christ in prayer and commanded the enemy to leave me alone. I was amazed at the result.

A short time later, a supervisor from another department saw what the woman was doing to me and was livid. She complained to the director of my department and the harassment stopped. It was beautiful to see how the Lord intervened on my behalf. Afterwards, whenever the woman would start to say something to me someone would take her aside and tell her to relax and calm down.

I am thankful that "in Christ" means I have a policeman's uniform on in the spirit. Evil spirits have no choice but to obey me when I say, "Stop!" because I have authority from the King. In other words—bullies beware. There is no weapon formed against me that will prosper.

"When Herod realized that he had been outwitted by the Magi, he was furious, and he gave orders to kill all the boys in Bethlehem and its vicinity who were two years old and under, in accordance with the time he had learned from the Magi."
(Matthew 2:16)

Other verses to look up: **Psalm 109:31, James 4:7**

Questions:

Are there any bullies in your life right now?(They don't have to be people. It could be in the area of your mind. Anxieties, relational conflicts, money problems, etc.)

Have you opened any doors (known sin) to let him into your life to harass you? If so, close the door through repentance (confess your sin and receive God's forgiveness through faith), submit to God, and command the devil and his cohorts out loud to leave you alone in Jesus' name. If you did not open a door to the enemy and you have a clean conscious before God, declare the same thing.

Praise the Lord in advance for His victory.

Hope For the Spiritually Challenged

One advantage of getting older is you can look back on your life—and those dumb things you did—and almost see the person who did them as someone else.

As odd as it may sound, my first revelation of "faith" came through a film with Barbra Streisand called *Funny Girl*. Of course, it had no connection with God, but the main character had an unshakable faith that one day she would be a "star" in the theatre.

Being a confirmed neurotic at the time, I wanted what she had—joy and faith in herself. Instead of being inspired, however, to find a direction for my life and go for it, I watched the film six times and became infatuated with Barbra Streisand.

Unfortunately, even after coming to Christ, I carried this obsession with me. I returned to college but figured it was only a holding tank until my real calling materialized. Like Fanny Brice in *Funny Girl,* nothing would stand in my way to greatness. It seemed natural, therefore, to jumpstart my career by doing a concert with Barbra.

To make my faith vision official I assembled my Christian friends at a local A & W for a meeting and announced my plans for a Carnegie Hall concert (with Babs) around frosty mugs of homemade root beer. They were shell-shocked with the news but afraid to dampen my faith with their incredulity.

Only George, the guy who built computers for the school Science Fairs and already had a real job that paid good money, saw things clearly: "Tim. You're nuts!"

I rebuked him openly for his lack of faith and used the famous phrase *God told me* to protect myself from any future balloon poppers.

With them or without them, I was going to pursue my dream. Had not God spoken? Somehow I learned the name and number of Barb's agent in California and gave him a call on my parents' phone. Amazingly, *(must be God, I thought)* I got through. A very confident man answered the phone. I began, "Ah, Marty. You don't know me but my name is Tim Bennett and I would like to do a concert with Barbra Streisand." He let me talk briefly and then became painfully pragmatic. "Ah . . . yeah. You want to do a concert with Barbra Streisand? So, how many albums have you done?" When I replied in the negative, he gently but firmly said to get some music recorded and send it right on out to him.

In my zeal I found his advice a little too much like work. I pressed on without a second thought. Somebody told me they knew someone who knew Elliot Gould, Streisand's ex-husband—an obvious green light from God even a spiritual moron could see. I called and explained what I wanted to do. The man was irate, "Do you know what people do for numbers like that?" When I didn't sound intimidated he gave me the name of a woman musician who had worked with

Barbra. His final words were haunting: "If you ever tell any-body where you got this number I'll seek you out and cut your tongue out." I gave him my address at college and shrugged off his Hollywood dramatics. I called the woman and we planned our rendezvous at the rock capital of the world—Woodstock.

When we finally connected, however, I realized I was-n't going to get what Joe Cocker would call "a little help from my friends." She explained she hadn't seen or worked with Barb "in ages." From there we digressed to talking about Barb's recent Barbara Walters interview on TV, like we were her closest pals. Finally, I pressed her for Barb's number. She replied, "It would take a lot of phone calls to get it." With the most velvet voice I could muster I asked, "Would you do that for me?" She said flatly, "No," and took the wind out of my sails for good. A perfect retort at the moment might have been: "Excuse me while I kiss the sky," borrowed from Jimi Hendrix, but instead I just said, "Oh . . . Okay," and walked away in a purple haze.

I thank God for his patience and His lifting of this delusional fog in my early days of walking with Him. I'm glad, too, that His promise in Philippians 1:6 is true regardless of how many times I fall on my face: *"Being confident of this very thing that He who began a good work in you will carry it on to com-pletion until the day of Christ Jesus."*

Other verses to look up: **1 Corinthians 10:12, Proverbs 24:16**

Questions:

Are you surprised sometimes by the types of people God calls?

(cont'd.)

Are there people in your church who seem a little odd or strange?

Take time now to pray for those people by name.

On Being a Twin

Throughout my life, I have heard people say with a tinge of mystery, "We all have a double somewhere in the world." Often the way it is said you half expect to hear Rod Serling's voice announce: *And welcome to . . . The Twilight Zone.*

To me, having a "double" or an identical twin, was nothing spooky—just life as I knew it and, at times, quite bothersome. Especially when other classmates would ask us over and over again: Who's tougher? Who's faster? Who's smarter? Who are *you* anyway?

Other times it could be amusing. Like the time I let Karen H., the redhead from one of Tom's classes, talk endlessly about something ridiculous that happened during their class. I remember patiently letting her finish her story, complete with animated hand movements and facial expressions, and then looking at her nonchalantly and saying, "I'm Tim." Her reaction took me by surprise. After a brief stunned silence, she screamed hysterically, in the middle of the drug store, "You beast! I'll never talk with you again!" This was probably the funniest thing of all because, as far as I could recollect, that was the first time our conversation had ever gone beyond, "Hi. Tom or Tim."

While we are at it, I would like to dispel a common myth about twins. They do not have extra sensory perception (ESP), which allows them to read one another's thoughts. The closest Tom and I ever came to that was one time when we invited the neighborhood kids over to our house for a "show." I pretended to be the "Great Carnac" and asked those in the audience to give their names and addresses very loudly and I would then guess their telephone numbers. Meanwhile, Tom was underneath a covered table with a telephone book looking up the numbers feverishly and whispering them up to me as I pushed my temples with my fingers like I was concentrating very hard.

Our jig was up when someone with an unlisted number yelled out his name and address. I think I may have blamed a passing cloud for the sudden static in my strange and wonderful *telepathetic* powers.

For the record, I will now answer the questions you have been dying to ask: Tom was more of a power hitter in baseball. He hit a homerun that sailed over the right field fence at Mrack camp. I never hit one, although I had a higher average when we were older. In bowling, I had the higher game and Tom the higher average. I was the better chess player. Tom could lift more weights, but I could usually out wrestle him. I beat Tom consistently in cross country runs in high school but he later excelled in long distance—after his stint in the army—and even won some amateur competitions. In ping-pong we were about equal.

So, what's the point in recounting all this? Be nice to a

twin. Get their name straight. Don't ask them the same questions all the time. And keep looking for your double in crowds and airports. You never know, they might want to switch places with you. Then again, you may be one of those people who don't care if there is anyone who looks like you in the world; you just want to have a character more like Jesus. If that's you, keep looking to:

> *". . . Jesus, the author and perfecter of our faith,*
> *who for the joy set before him endured the cross, scorning its shame,*
> *and sat down at the right hand of the throne of God."*
> **(Hebrews 12:2)**

Other verses to look up: **Psalm 139**

Questions:

How do you feel after reading this psalm?

Do you feel unique and secure in God's love and plan for your life?

Marriage is an Oyster

Over the centuries, poets and songwriters have compared holy matrimony to many things. One popular song goes like this: "Love and marriage. Love and marriage. Go together like a horse and carriage." Though it may rhyme, this ditty does little to shed light on this noble and time-honored institution.

The oyster, in my opinion, is the perfect analogy for the marriage relationship. *"Why an oyster?"* you may ask. First of all, an oyster has a hard shell. Like it or not, marriage is hard in many ways. It demands discipline. You are expected to remain faithful to your partner for a lifetime. You are also expected to work out your conflicts within its framework.

Unfortunately, what hinders the blossoming of a marriage relationship is the dumb notion that you come into your marriage with a perfect love and you are to maintain this intensity forever. This is far from the truth. Often we come into this relationship from a self-centered point of view and, more times than not, our love is based more on emotional infatuation than unconditional love.

A better way to enter this covenant relationship is with the idea that your love is imperfect and will need a lifetime to mature with the help of your mate and the grace of God.

In the life of an oyster, even a grain of sand can interrupt its daily functioning. Yet, rather than rejecting this foreign particle, the oyster forms a pearl by covering it with a homemade substance. Precious pearls can take many years before they are recognized for their value. So it is in the marriage relationship. When something comes into the relationship that seems foreign and strange, couples can call upon the grace and covering of God to come to bear on the situation or the individual. After many years even those from the outside can see what this couple possesses is something very precious indeed.

Sometimes the grain of sand in the marriage can simply be the personality difference of the spouse. As we all know, opposite personalities attract like magnets. When the personalities are extremely different this can cause constant friction and conflict. Yet, the reason we are attracted to opposite personalities in the first place is because we often lack the positive character trait inherent in the other personality. Unconsciously, we probably desire what that other person has to be incorporated into our characters so that we will be more complete as individuals. If we refuse to grow in that particular area when conflicts arise we may begin to resent the very characteristic that drew us together initially.

A typical combination of giftings and personality combinations in the marriage relationship can be the #1 Combo of Pastor/Prophet (sweet and sour) mix. The pastor personality would be one that enjoys peace between people, is easy-going, relaxed, dislikes confrontation, and is generally optimistic.

The prophet type, however, thrives on the truth regardless of who gets hurt, sees long-term implications, and is, perhaps, more in tune with reality. For example, suppose a windfall of unexpected money comes into the family. The pastor type immediately sees all the things he has wanted to buy and figures now is the time to do it.

The prophet counters this thinking with a reminder of all the bills that are due that very month such as the rent, utilities, phone, and the credit card leaving roughly $1.50—that might be enough to buy a sundae at McDonald's.

A situation like this, if not handled delicately, could explode into WWIII. The pastor personality feels like he or she is in a straitjacket by constant fiscal restraints and sees the money influx as a way to breath again. The prophet type, on the other hand, sees the money as a Godsend just to cover basic expenses. If the problem is examined by the two in a calm objective manner, they may find that both parties are justified in their thinking. One exaggerates what money is really available and the other exaggerates the expenses (maybe trying to cover them too far down the road). A compromise could be a special night out at a restaurant or to a special event that both could enjoy instead of a new computer, car, and wardrobe.

I repeat. Marriage is not a carriage but an oyster. Don't let those inevitable grains of sand that come into your relationship be a source of irritation and resentment, but an opportunity to mature your love into a pearl of great price. And don't be surprised if this doesn't happen overnight.

Other verses to look up: **Hebrews 13:4; 1 Corinthians 13**

(cont'd.)

Questions:

What are your ideas of love and where did they come from?

Are they based on the Word of God or on Hollywood's version of love?

How do these two points of view differ?

Is love just a feeling? If so, what happens when the feelings are not there?

How can you know if you truly love someone?

In Love or Infatuated?

When I saw Michelle in my music theory class I was smitten. She had long dark hair, wore long dresses, played guitar and sang, plus she even wore boots. That may not turn on many guys these days but each generation has its mode of dress and back in the '70s this was a common young woman's statement of I-am-my-own-person-with-something-to-say garb. The fact that she wasn't a Christian didn't deter me. Since I was new to the faith myself I took this as a challenge rather than a "No Trespassing" sign. Thus, I pursued her, got her to say a prayer of conversion, and then discovered something—it's not fun seeing a mirror image of yourself. For example, she was very competitive in chess, bowling, and even music like I was. When she lost at the games she would sulk, like me, and even take the joy out of my winning, which was particularly irritating. She also, much to my chagrin, did not disband her folk group with two other guys, as I had suggested, and simply sing with me. Eventually, I saw the futility of a long-term relationship with her. Our personalities were just too much alike to be of help to one another—plus the fact her slippery spiritual path was beset with compromise.

Other romantic interludes included a young woman, Caroline, from England with a terrific accent, and an eccentric artist with a Russian name. The English lass told me one day I was in the top three. The friend who introduced me to her was also in the line-up, too, although she didn't tell me his exact position. His standing became crystal clear one day as I was singing to her the classic song by Neil Diamond, "Sweet Caroline." Apparently, she was so captivated by my singing she had trouble looking up from the letter she was writing to our "mutual" friend. This time, however, I got the not-so-subtle message and dropped her like a tea bag in the Boston harbor.

The artist love interest was original. She described me as a "potted plant" and another suitor as "flashes of light." Again, it wasn't too hard to guess which one she preferred. In a way, she confirmed my pastoral gifting, that I was a caring kind of guy, but also made it appear a little boring. The "flashes of light" fellow apparently had a radio program where he gushed biblical revelation like a fire hydrant. That same day, when I least expected it, she came up to me while I was in the kitchen and gave me a passionate kiss on the mouth. When I asked her, "What was that for?" she replied, "I just wanted to see something." I figured I didn't do too well on the kissing Richter scale when she told me later, "You're not the one." (I mean, what can you expect from a plant?) Not wanting to waste the experience, though, I wrote a poem rivaling Shakespeare called, "Perhaps."*

But why am I telling you all this? Well, there are two ways of learning things. One is through our own painful

*See page 88

experience; another way, infinitely less costly, is learning from others. Through the course of time, I discovered the best way to distinguish between infatuation and love is to honestly answer the following questions:

Do you feel at ease with this person and accepted for who you are, or, do you have to pretend to be someone else?

Are you friends with this person or merely a romantic interest?

Do you really know this person or are you just projecting onto them who you would like them to be?

Are you blind to some major character defects that everyone else can see?

Do people who know you think this is a good match?

Does this person really want to follow Jesus or is God only a side issue?

Are you willing to cut off this relationship if Jesus says no?

Now . . . are you in love or in infatuation?

Deep down you know the truth.

"Do not arouse or awaken love until it so desires."
(Song of Songs 3:5b)

Perhaps

Perhaps you'll find this fellow you've created in your mind
A perfect blend of color camouflaged in time.
On a steed some day, armor shining, he'll gallop into view
And sweep you up bedazzled enamored by his hue.

Perhaps he'll take you up to castles seldom seen
Avoiding rocky crags and jumping every stream.
Maybe many magic magi you'll be privileged to meet
Who'll prostrate fall like a foe beneath his stirrupped feet.

Perhaps in time you'll weary of this long and harried pace
Imagining a meadow and his warm embrace.
But this man of your fancy cannot stop nor turn around
The metal that he wears serves solely to weigh him down.

Perhaps this knight, with all his armor, cannot play his part
For you've hidden what is human and galvanized his heart.

Memories of My Father

I was 22 and waiting in the hospital emergency room when they wheeled the bed with my father on it into view. He looked up and said weakly, "Good-bye Buddy." Little did I know at the time that those words would be the last he would ever say to me. I had just returned from California a few months earlier in 1975 as a prodigal son who now had faith, but I had no idea how close dad was to the end. He was only 57 and had been battling cancer of the colon for two years while I was fighting my own battle with God on the other side of the country.

He had always been a very responsible kind of guy—a former officer in the Navy, a district claims manager for Nationwide Insurance, the chairman of the local Republican Party, and our faithful baseball coach during little league and Babe Ruth.

His disciplinary practices, however, could be very unorthodox. For example, one day when he smelled smoke in my room, he sat me down at the dining room table and had me smoke a cigar. When I reached the end he gave me a toothpick so I could really finish it completely. I thought I would be a wise guy and began inhaling the smoke and letting it come out through my nose. Later, on the baseball field, while he was hitting my twin brother and I "high flies" I became very sick to my stomach. Consequently, cigarettes never became a habit for me.

I always remember him smiling and being friendly to people, even those who would not even acknowledge his greetings.

When we received the Nationwide Insurance magazine after his death it included a page of over 20 quotes about him from people who knew him best at work. Here are a few:

> *"One of the kindest and most understanding people I have ever met."*
> *"He had a certain ease about him that drew people to him."*
> *"Genuine love for people."*
> *"He was the greatest person I ever met or worked for."*
> *"Always aware that those working for him were people first and subordinates second."*

I'll never forget one heavyset co-worker who came to the wake. He looked me straight in the eye, on the verge of tears, and said with deep conviction, "Your father was a wonderful man."

I was touched that people loved him and yet, the most I could say was, "Dad, I hardly knew ya."

I knew part of the reason was my own. I let myself get sucked into the rebellious generation of the '60s and '70s that openly defied all forms of authority—parental included. Despite all my ranting and raving, though, I knew something was desperately wrong with me that needed to change. In the hopes of "finding myself" through Primal Therapy (endorsed by Beatle John Lennon) I took a Greyhound with my girlfriend to Los Angeles. Instead of finding inner peace, however, I discovered my hatred erupted from bottomless depths. Later, a young man explained to me the way to have a personal relationship with God through Jesus Christ.

After my marriage, when my wife and I adopted a baby boy, whom we named Samuel after the biblical prophet, feelings of sadness would pop up at strange times. One time when I was trying to fix our toilet, Sammy put on his plastic tool belt and came to see if he could help me out. Later that night tears flowed freely as I thought about how innocent and precious Sammy's love was for me, his dad—something I once had for my own father but which had eventually died from lack of nourishment.

Another time, after a men's retreat, I found myself driving in the car and suddenly needing to find a place to be alone so I could weep over the loss of a father/son relationship that never was and never could be. No. He had never abused me; he wasn't an alcoholic; and he had never committed adultery. We just never got to know one another very well. When I found an empty park along side the road, I must have cried for over an hour. It had been 20 years since his death and I had never really grieved over this lack in my life. This time, however, it seemed like a right kind of grief—not from resentment or anger but from a legitimate need left unmet.

Today, I make it a priority to spend time with my children individually and to read stories to them and ask them about their days. It is not always easy and, at times, I need to remind myself of my commitment. I was encouraged recently, though, when a person who works with children said, "You have very special relationships with your son and daughter that I don't see very often."

I may not be able to leave a large financial inheritance to my children when I go, but one legacy I want them to always carry in their hearts is: My daddy loved me. I know because he took time to be with me.

"We love because He first loved us."
(1 John 4:19)

Another verse to look up: **Malachi 4:5-6**

Questions:

What is the best time you remember spending with your dad? (Dads and Moms can share their best experiences with their fathers).

What are the things you like (or liked if he is no longer alive) to do best with your dad?

The Man Who Beat the Gladiators

If one was to guess how the gladiators were finally eradicated from Rome, one may falsely assume from the film, *Gladiator,* that it was by someone stronger and better than all the others—like its hero, "Maximus," who carved up opponents at will, regardless of size and weaponry, like Thanksgiving turkeys.

History, however, reveals quite a different story with a very different kind of man. The truth is, an obscure monk named Telemachus was the one responsible for stopping the so-called "games."

But before revealing how he did it, let's look at the decadence of Rome the day of Telemachus' arrival. According to accounts by the ancient historian Procopius, Rome had won its last victory over the Goths. To celebrate the triumph, thousands flocked to the coliseum to watch the customary chariot races and gladiator fights.

As usual, all of the gladiators that day were marched around the arena and finally before the Emperor's stand, where they yelled out in unison with hands raised: "Hail, Caesar! Those about to die salute thee!" Afterwards they found themselves in a fight-to-the-death struggle with one of the unfortunates next to them—armed often with only a three-pronged spear and net, or a sword.

The fights also had their traditions. For example, when one of the gladiators pinned his opponent, the victor would look up to the stands for a thumb's up or a thumb's down from his fans. Up meant he was to spare the loser while a thumb's down meant, "Kill him!" If that wasn't enough to show their cold-heartedness, it got worse. If a victim resisted the final deathblow they would begin to chant, "Receive the steel! Receive the steel!" meaning he should give his neck for the blade. Hooks were then used to drag the corpse from the arena as attendants covered his blood trail with fresh sand for the next contestants.

It was in the midst of this callous environment that something totally unheard of took place. Suddenly, in the middle of a match, a man clad in a coarse-looking hooded robe climbed into the arena and boldly approached two of the battling gladiators. He placed his hand on one of them and reproached him for attempting to shed innocent blood. He then turned to the stunned crowd and yelled out in a solemn deep-toned voice that echoed throughout the stadium, "Do not requite God's mercy in turning away the swords of your enemies by murdering each other!"

Instead of receiving the rebuke, however, the crowd became infuriated and urged the gladiators to continue their contest. "The old traditions of Rome must be observed!" they screamed. Despite the protests, the man remained standing between the gladiators and tried to reason again with the belligerent mob. The din of angry voices shouted, "Down with him!" and the gladiators' swords quickly silenced his earnest appeals forever. After he had fallen he was pelted with rocks and any other object that the spectators could find.

Not much is known about Telemachus. His robe was that of a hermit who had vowed himself to prayer and self-denial. The few who knew him said he had come from Asia on a pilgrimage to visit churches and to celebrate Christmas in Rome.

His offense at the horrifying way the people were entertaining themselves and dishonoring God pushed him into an action that cost him his life.

His death, however, saved many lives. Apparently convicted by the words of the martyr, the emperor, from that day forward, never allowed gladiator fights in the coliseum again.

> *"But God demonstrates his own love for us in this:*
> *While we were still sinners, Christ died for us."*
> **(Romans 5:8)**

Other verses to look up: **2 Samuel 23:13-17**

Question:

In your opinion, what is unconditional love?

Can you think of someone you know who doesn't like you?

Project:

Do something nice for this person this week.

What Do You Do With Ten Grand?

When I first found out that I won first prize and $10,000 in the national Amy Awards, it was hard to sleep or keep my mind on simple tasks. I was too busy coming up with ideas on how to spend the money—retirement fund, deposit on a house, a new computer, trip to Italy, ad nauseam. In fact, I talked about it so much my wife eventually commented, "Couldn't we talk about something else?" to which I replied, "But . . . but . . . how often do you win ten thousand dollars for one article! Shouldn't we talk about how to spend it?"

It was then I figured I'd better spend a little more time praying about it and actively listening to the Lord. There must be a reason the Lord was giving this money to us at this time. What could it be? Did He want us to put down roots somewhere in France by buying a house? The answer, however, seemed elusive.

One day while I was praying again on the subject, a question came to mind: *Why don't you adopt another child?* My immediate reaction was: *Whaaaaat! Are you kidding?* In fact many times I felt I had my hands full just refereeing conflicts between my young son and daughter. I could see myself qualifying for a position with the World Wrestling and Boxing Associations, but take another child into our family . . . *I don't know about that, Lord. This cannot be You, can it?*

Then I remembered Véronique's dream to have an international family with children from different nations and how, even with natural childbirth, children can come when you least expect them. I prayed, nonetheless, and put out a fleece before the Lord: *Lord, if this idea is from You, have someone talk about adoption at the YWAM conference in Budapest, Hungary when we go there.* I mean, c'mon, what are the odds that someone will talk about adoptions at a missionary conference?

When we arrived at the conference, I was curious what workshops were being offered. We were interested in church planting and had signed up for this workshop. Instead, the speaker for this subject didn't show up, and there was a workshop on, you guessed it, international adoptions. I explained what had happened to the director of the adoption agency who was speaking and she said, "Sounds like God to me." I immediately said I needed more than just one confirmation on something as radical and life-changing as this decision. I told Véronique about my fleece and she said, "Well, that's the first thing you've mentioned that excites me."

Still, I needed more proof. I tried to reason with the Lord: *Lord, you know I'm going on 50. It's not exactly the best time to have small children, is it?* And, like all good Bible-believing Christians, I wanted some biblical confirmation so I prayed that the Lord would give me something from the Word. Some time later, we decided to go to a small church in another town about 10 minutes from where we lived. There might have been 10 people there including the four of us. It was one of those churches where the pastor was doing everything—the welcome, the worship, the offering, and the message. I turned to the sermon text in the Gospel of John. My eyes drifted to a verse on the opposite page that read: *"I will not leave you as orphans; I will come to you"* (John 14:18).

Another confirmation came when I arrived in Lansing, Michigan where I was to receive my check at an annual prayer breakfast. While riding in the car with the president of the Amy Foundation, James Russell, who would be giving me my award, I turned to him and said, "Wouldn't it be interesting to find out what the other first prize winners did with their money and if their lives were changed in any way?" Keeping his eyes on the road he said nonchalantly, "Funny you should say that 'if their lives changed,' because one winner's life really changed—he adopted a child." And, if these confirmations weren't enough, Véronique and I were attending another seminar on the family and the speaker said, "He that receives a child, receives the Lord." I asked Véronique later if she was thinking what I was thinking and she, of course, said the adoption was the first thing that came to mind.

Our next step was to share our plans with our two children, Alicia and Samuel. Their response was, "Why don't we adopt two children, one boy and one girl." It was at this juncture that Véronique began to pray earnestly. During one of her quiet times she was reading in Acts where Phillip was in the middle of revival in Samaria when he was suddenly taken to a "desert road" to minister to the Ethiopian eunuch. Véronique felt impressed that Phillip had been in the middle of "ministry" when he was called to minister to one man. She was convinced this was the word of the Lord about our adoption. We were to adopt one child.

In retrospect, we can see why so many confirmations were necessary. The application process, though shorter than many, was long—it took one year and was very complicated because of the fact we were both from different countries and living in France. The ordeal in the Ukraine was also not easy. We had to go to the national bureau of adoptions in Kiev and choose one child among thousands. When we saw the photo of a boy with a sad face our hearts went out to him. I asked if he was available for adoption. The woman said, "Sorry, there is another couple looking at him right now and he will probably be adopted soon." We decided to go with our gut feelings. "When will you know if he will be adopted?" "Tomorrow." "Okay, then we will wait until tomorrow." Sure enough, the couple, who really wanted a girl, decided not to adopt the boy which left him available for us. We took the children to see him for a week and they adopted him into their hearts as they played with him and tried to communicate with him despite the language barrier. We named him Jonathan. It has now been more than two years and little Johnny has made gigantic strides forward. He now speaks and reads in French and understands English. Over the last couple of months we have been encouraged that even people from outside our family have seen how much he has blossomed since he first came to us. We are convinced that he, as well as our other children, has a specific destiny in God and we are praying that He will discover it and pursue it with all his heart.

Other verses to look up: **John 10:27, 1 Kings 19:12**

Questions:

Do you allow time to listen to God in prayer? If so, when was the last time you believe God said something specifically to you?

Project:

Spend time being quiet before God during the next week and then share as a family what God said to you. He may tell you to do something for someone you know, your family, friends, or someone who is an acquaintance. He might just use a Bible verse to encourage you. Be open and believe God will speak to you. If you believe He has said something, be obedient to what He said (always be sure, or course, that the action does not conflict with what the Bible says is right).

Elijah Therapy: A Cure for the Driven

I sat alone at a round table, unconsciously inhaling the musty smell of old books, in the college library feverishly trying to polish off another healthy dose of higher education homework when I just happened to look up and see Chris. He was sitting at the table in front of me. Apparently, he had finished his required work early and was now simply reading for fun. He looked comfortable and cozy in a clean dark blue sweater. I saw the profile of his face and distinctly saw a slight smile on his lips like he had been chuckling to himself. He had dark hair, modern frameless glasses, and straight white teeth. I envied him. He received straight As in all his courses and had the discipline and brains to work hard at the course work and then relax and enjoy learning what he wanted to—like taking a slow meandering walk on the first warm day of Spring. I wondered what it must feel like not to have that monkey of obligation on your shoulder. As one of the "older" students who had returned to school after four years off, I found it hard just getting my assignments done on time. I also worked evenings as a dishwasher in a busy Italian restaurant. Therefore, I constantly felt like a juggler who had to keep two balls up in the air while he caught one. Chris, however, was different. He had learned something that would take me years to learn—how not to feel guilty when you relax.

Unfortunately as Christians, we sometimes become so busy doing the Lord's work that we don't take the time to do something we like to do. I discovered how driven I was a number of years ago when I had an appendectomy. When the nurse came into my room in the hospital and said, "You'll have to stay in the hospital for a few days," I couldn't help myself—I was thrilled.

Normally you wouldn't think a person would relish the idea of staying in a hospital but I was so tired in all departments (emotionally, mentally, and spiritually), I welcomed the break. This way I could get my needed rest without feeling guilty. After all, I didn't volunteer to stay in the hospital—they forced me. The decision was beyond my control. That meant no pressures nor responsibilities for a few days. All I had to do was sleep, eat, and roll over now and then for a shot. My only responsibility was resting and receiving care from others while I healed.

As I reflected on this type of "therapy" I realized that there was even a model for this in the Bible. Elijah had given the word of the Lord to King Ahab that it would not rain for a few years in 1 Kings 17. Just after this, God instructs Elijah to: *"Leave here, turn eastward and hide in the Kerith Ravine, east of the Jordan. You will drink from the brook, and I have ordered the ravens to feed you there."* In other words, "Elijah, I am going to make you lie down in green pastures. You won't have to do any-thing but eat and sleep and you won't even have to be concerned about where your meals are coming from." The Lord knew that giving the word of the Lord sometimes can weigh heavily on the person who gives it—especially when the consequences could mean his own termination. He knows, too, when we are overworking ourselves and not giving attention to our personal needs.

I have found if I don't allow time in my weekly schedule to do something I enjoy, just for the sake of enjoying it, I develop an attitude toward God that He is a harsh and demanding Person who always expects more than I can give. If I keep this negative attitude long enough I also become judgmental of others if they aren't doing all the "work" of the Lord that I am doing.

For some of us this short break from the pressures and routines of life may be a walk in the woods, or to read a few chapters of a good book, or to call someone we haven't talked to in a while, rather than always "sticking to the schedule." When we take a special moment during the day to simply delight in the Lord by doing something we like to do, it is surprising how God can renew us in His peace and joy. It's a wonderful feeling when we realize that the weight of the world shouldn't be on our shoulders anyway, but on Jesus who asks us to cast all our cares upon Him.

Don't wait for an appendectomy to learn this one. If someone tries to push you into something that you don't have the grace to handle, just tell them you are in "Elijah Therapy" —maybe you'll get a chance to explain what that means and save someone else from a "driven" way of life.

*Other verses to look up: **Ecclesiastes 5:19, Hebrews 4:9***

(cont'd.)

Questions:

What hobbies do you have that help you to relax?

Do you plan these activities into your weekly/daily schedule?

Do you respect those moments when other family members are taking some down time?

Maybe you have another problem—you let others do most of the work while you are often playing and having fun. Which one are you and how can you have a better balance between "all work and no play" and "all play and no work"?

All for a Glance at Lance
(Tour de France 2002)

After reading the e-mail from a lawyer friend, Joe, from the States, I figured I had to do it. He was sending his lovely 15-year-old girl, Abby, to visit with us in the south of France and the dates coincided exactly with the Tour de France.

Joe simply put two and two together on his computer—Mount Ventoux and our home town of St. Paul 3 Châteaux—and bingo. "The Tour de France will be passing right near where you live!" he wrote enthusiastically. "You gotta go see it!"

Of course, I knew Mount Ventoux was one of those hills out yonder but, to be honest, I had trouble getting excited about watching guys in fancy spandex uniforms riding bikes.

After three years in France, I still have not understood the French fascination with watching the Tour de France. Yes, it is a French sport on French soil and there is always the eternal hope that a French man will win (and they say the French don't believe in God) but what is interesting about watching jerky images (taken from motorcycles) of the same panting guys on bikes for weeks battling for a yellow tee shirt?

Yet, while in Marseilles on business last year, almost every bar I passed had the Tour de France on TV whether anyone was watching it or not. Out of curiosity, I would just duck in for a couple of minutes to ask, "How's Lance doing?" to which someone would inevitably mutter, "Yes. Still in front."

Now I was committed. On the day of the Mount Ventoux ascent, it was hot. With my wife, Véronique, my three kids, and Abby in our Peugeot 405, the car was crowded. No air conditioning. The hour and a half ride was not fun. The kids began bleating at various intervals, "When will we be there?"

Abby remained polite. Remember she was on a mission from dad. She was also a stranger in a strange land. She was also being fed and housed by us. Her determined facial expression, despite her sardine-like body position, meant she would endure to the end, come what may, and report back to her dad, "I did it."

Finally, we arrived at the little village the cyclists would pass through on their way to the summit. Unfortunately, thousands of others lined both sides of the road. Vendors of Tour de France hats and shirts, drinks, and other assorted trinkets, were busy selling their wares. Spots of shade were hard to come by. Jonathan, our seven-year-old, complained of fatigue. I hoisted him onto my shoulders but after 3.5 meters my back began to complain.

We stopped when we saw openings in the line. We waited for hours. Did I say it was hot? Words came down the line that the forerunner vehicles to the Tour de France were coming. Another hour passes. Then, all of a sudden, scores of custom-made vehicles came whipping buy us in various shapes, some representing products. Some had people in them that threw things out at the crowds—candy, coffee, ice cream, little toys, bottled water, newspapers. They must have depleted much of their samples in other towns because we had slim pickings. Some cars and vans sprayed people with water.

I decided to go to the other side of the street near a curve. I told my family to yell when they saw a guy in a yellow shirt. The cheers were getting closer. "Now!" they all screamed. I snapped the photo. Seconds later they were gone. We retraced our route for another hour and a half in a hot non-air-conditioned car.

The next day, vowing to never to go see a Tour de France again under my breath, I noticed some photographers gathering outside my office building. I asked the guy nearest me, who worked for an Italian magazine, sporting a huge camera neck ornament, what was going on. He said, "The U.S. Postal team is due to arrive in a couple of minutes." Forgetting my seconds' old resolution, I quickly dashed all the way back to my apartment, up the three flights of stairs two steps at a time, to get my camera, and back down. As I was running back up to the main road I saw glimpses of the U.S. Postal team passing. I didn't see Lance. I waved but nobody waved back. Out of breath I made it back to where the reporters were. The only person talking with the reporters was the coach. I waited and waited. They said Lance was inside eating lunch with the team. Can we go in there? "No." Oh. Will they come back out? "Maybe." I waited some more.

Several minutes later a guy shows up on his bike, apparently far behind the other team members. A few reporters talk with him. He looks familiar but I can't place him.

It looks like he's cracking a few jokes. He hangs out a while enjoying a few pictures with people. A woman next to me says, "I just had my photo taken with Robin Williams!" Right. So, that's who it is. I figure I'll implement a line from one of his movies and "carpe diem." I snap a couple of photos.

In looking at my roll of film later, Lance is not there but, as if by magic, Peter Pan is, in living color sporting a U.S. Postal team uniform. Hey, it wasn't exactly what I wanted but, like my dad used to say, "it sure beats a stick in the eye."

"And I saw that all labor and all achievement
spring from man's envy of his neighbor.
This too is meaningless, a chasing after the wind."
(Ecclesiastes 4:4)

Another verse to look up: **Mark 8:36**

Questions:

Have you ever greatly anticipated something and been greatly disappointed?

Did you learn anything from this experience?

Someone once said, "Our disappointments are God's appointments." What do you think this means?

The Angst of Being an Artist

If you are not an artist of any kind you are probably wondering what the word "angst" means. If so, I will wait until you look it up . . . Stop. I know you'd rather skip this article than go find a dictionary. I'll do it for you. Here we go. "Angst," according to Webster's College Dictionary of 1991, means "a feeling of dread, anxiety, or anguish." You may ask, "Why do artists experience this? What's the matter with them? Can't they just buck up and take the flack of life like everyone else? Why do they have to be so sensitive any way?"

The fact that most writers (artists, musicians, actors) tend to be thin-skinned is because if they didn't feel strongly about something they probably would never write or do anything creative. It is the fact they have been indelibly marked by an experience or idea that pushes them to express themselves in some imaginative way. The passion for their subject also helps them get through the long, and sometimes painful, creative process.

Along with this sensitivity, most writers and artists

also have a compelling need to communicate to others what they have created. Some writers may deceive themselves by saying they only write for themselves but then, why did they tell you about it?

Yet, with many creative projects the writer must confront "angst" because it is difficult to be objective about one's own work. A writer must, therefore, put aside what others may think and simply do the best he can. During this period it is not unusual to feel like a pilot caught in a heavy fog. If he looks around he may panic and feel totally lost, not knowing if he is flying upside down or right side up. The only thing that keeps him going is his instrument panel.

For the writer, the only indicator that he is on the right track may be his own gut feeling. His hope is that, as he continues, the fog will lift and he will eventually see where to land. Doubts can assail his thoughts in mid-flight, like: *What if I am just cursed with a mediocre talent and this is all in vain?*

For columnists, it can be even worse since readership is hard to evaluate and feedback sometimes nonexistent. For all they know, the only reason they are being published is because the editor likes their writing (which is wonderful, but not so great if they are the only ones) or, on bad days, they may think it is printed just to fill a blank space.

On really dark days they may even question if their articles are read at all, or if it is just used for flooring for parakeet cages. (I don't mind this as long as my column is read first and the airspace over my photo is a no-fly zone).

Writers can be comforted, however, by the fact that many successful authors have had these doubts, too, even after winning prestigious literary awards. They include Bodie Thoene, Neil Simon, Art Buchwald, Ernest Hemingway, and

John Steinbeck.

The ultimate question that each writer must answer on his own, despite his "angst," is: Has God called me to write? If he or she can answer that with a resounding "Yes!" he will write no matter what worldly success or influence he has achieved.

Yet, writers are human, too, and could use a little encouragement now and then.

> *"An anxious heart weighs a man down,*
> *but a kind word cheers him up."*
> **(Proverbs 12:25)**

Questions:

Have you appreciated something you read this week in a newspaper, magazine, or book?

Family project:

Why not send a letter to that writer today and let them know specifically what you liked about it?

Retirement Ideas for Pastors and Counselors

In this new millennium I think we should think about new ways of making a living. I thought of a good job, especially for freelance pastors and counselors, called a Family Communications Consultant. This position would be ideal for those who've worked in the "people" business for a number of years. The FCC would be a guy or gal who comes into the family for 90 days or so and just observes how the family functions. Before he comes in, however, every member of the family must sign a contract that they will accept the evidence presented by the FCC and not resort to derogatory name-calling or fruit-throwing of any kind.

Practically, the FCC would normally occupy an unobtrusive corner of the room wherever the family happens to be. He would be equipped with nothing more than a pad of paper and a small cassette player to record all interactions between family members. He would provide his own meals and promise not to make too much noise as to be distracting to the normal family discourses. For example, he would be forbidden from eating such foods as raw carrots, celery, soup, potato chips, etc. which may draw attention to himself.

At the end of the three-month period, the family would gather around the table for the "Family Round-Up" and the FCC would address each family member individually in the presence of the others. To lighten the mood of the disclosures, the family could wear western clothes like boots, cowboy hats, kerchiefs, and the like. A copy of the evidence would be given to each family member and also kept on file at the FCC's office in case of frequent memory lapses.

To give you an idea of what the "Family Round-Up" would be like, I'll illustrate it with a few samplings from a FRU with a family we'll call the Bennetts:

FCC: Mr. Bennett. Thank you for being the brave one to go first. Since you are paying me by the hour and your eyes will naturally drift to the clock above us periodically, we will get right into it . . . Isn't it true that you asked your wife 119 times for things that were right in front of your nose, such as the juice, the butter in the fridge, your wallet, your brown sweater, during the last 90 days? And isn't it true, one time you even yelled to the other end of the house questioning where your glasses were when, in fact, they were pushed up on top of your head? And isn't it true, Mr. Bennett, that you said 15 times during the first week alone that you wanted to lose 10 pounds and patted your belly in front of the mirror daily, but, in fact, you took three helpings on all but two of your meals, ate the remaining pieces of pizza when you thought no one was looking, consumed seven Snickers bars, and scoffed down five glazed donuts? And, isn't it true, Mr. Bennett, that you drove your car to the store on May 23 when it was only a five minute walk by foot? And, isn't it true, Mr. Bennett, that once in the store, you jumped into the motorized cart, normally for senior citizens, and raced to the various aisles, even grabbing a video in passing that section—another passive activity, I might add—which only encourages snack consumption and reduces your mind to mush? Would you like to see the photos that prove these findings Mr. Bennett?

Mr. Bennett: Ah no. That won't be necessary but, ah . . . (now whispering to the FCC) Excuse me, Sir, but for a little extra could we delete a few of these from the official report?

FCC: I am sorry Mr. Bennett, but your bribe just cost you an additional $50. Thank you. May I continue?

Mr. Bennett: (clearing his throat) Yes. Most certainly.

FCC: Mrs. Bennett. I have you on tape asking your husband to do a variety of things in rapid succession even before he had time to complete one of your requests. You also complained about not being able to drive the car sometimes. Yet, when your husband let you drive you had so many things on the floor on the passenger side such as a cosmetic bag, purse, snacks for the children, and the picnic cooler, that he couldn't comfortably put his feet down without crushing a multitude of items. You also said on 32 occasions that you were ready to go when in fact you took another 12 to 30 minutes to get out the door. Isn't it true, Mrs. Bennett?

Mrs. Bennett: 12 to 30 minutes seems like a gross exaggeration to me. May I listen to the evidence please?

FCC: Of course. (They now listen to one hour of sounds in the Bennett household on a typical Sunday morning. Sounds of many footsteps are heard going up and down a hallway, a refrigerator door opening and closing, liquids being poured into glasses, and children alternately giggling and fighting with one another. At the moment Mrs. Bennett says, "I'm ready" the FCC punches the stop clock he has pulled out of his pocket. When the sound of a closing door is heard, the FCC stops the watch.)

Mrs. Bennett: But that was only 28 minutes.

FCC: Yes, Mrs. Bennett. You are technically correct but if you will kindly turn to page 24 of our contract it says that we can round off to the nearest five minutes. May I continue?

Mrs. Bennett: Yes.

FCC: Hi there little fella. Are you ready for your assessment?

Samuel: Do you have any chocolate?

FCC: I am very sorry but I don't eat it during business hours. Now Samuel, isn't it true that you excused yourself on April 3rd from the dinner table for presumably to use the bathroom but, in fact, you spit your green beans in the sink and then let them float down the drain? Yet, when the plumber was called to fix the blocked sink and consequently removed the soggy vegetables, only then did you confess to the crime. And, isn't it true . . .

Samuel: Daddy, why does that man look so mean and use such funny words?

Mr. Bennett: (under his breath to Sammy) That's because he watches too many *Perry Mason* re-runs on TV and doesn't eat chocolate during his business hours. What he wants to know is why you were dishonest to Mommy and Daddy and spit your green beans in the sink instead of eating them?

FCC: So you see this as wrong, Samuel?

Samuel: If I get caught (looking at his dad's frown). Yes.

FCC: Thank you. Now about your conversations. You obviously are obsessed with burps and other bodily eruptions. In fact, you mentioned them 467 times in the space of three days and accused your dad 40 times of having done these acts when, in fact, they hadn't transpired more than 29 times. Isn't it true?

> *Samuel:* Daddy, can I have some chocolate?

> *FCC* and *Dad:* (in unison) No.

We will end here. As you can see the job is not easy and, in fact, can be quite frustrating especially when you know the truth but nobody acknowledges it. Of course, in reality, you cannot have this position of FCC. It is already filled by the THS: The Holy Spirit. The real question is: Is anybody listening?

> *"But when he, the Spirit of truth, comes,*
> *he will guide you into all truth."*
> **(John 16:13)**

Other verses to look up: **John 3:19-21**

Questions:

Is there anything the Holy Spirit may be saying to you recently that you are not hearing for some reason (maybe even through someone else in the family)?

Why do people sometimes choose to ignore the Holy Spirit in their lives?

Back to the Basics

"**J**ump!" screamed a man in a garbage truck out of the passenger window as he whizzed beneath the overpass. I had been leaning over the railing and seriously thinking of letting gravity take me into the busy traffic below. Here I was—22 years old, 3,000 miles away from home, and without hope for my life. How had a Protestant-raised easterner come to such a point of desperation?

If you remember, the period of the late '60s and early '70s was an era of great soul-searching. As a generation we were convinced we were sick, neurotic, and in need of something. How else could all those wild therapies in California have attracted so many? Sex therapy, Gestalt therapy, EST, group therapy. You name it and there was probably a therapy for it.

For me, as for many others (on the East Coast anyway), California represented the Promised Land. Get away from what you're used to and you'll be free. Far from parents, old friends, old situations. After all, it's the environment that makes you the way you are. Change the environment and you'll change.

The problem with my philosophy, though, was simple. I couldn't leave myself behind with all the rest. But my plan went beyond just geographical location. At the suggestion of my older brother, I had read a book in college, *The Primal Scream,* and it gave me some focus for my life. The book confirmed my suspicions that I was neurotic and in need of help. The method to escape, the author explained, was to release all the feelings you'd suppressed as a child in what he called "primals." These occurred when you reached the core of the emotion you were ventilating. They could all be reduced to screaming or wailing. Some patients were even reported to have re-experienced their emergence from the womb. I wasn't very intrigued by this experience, but the small print under the book's title gave me all the hope I needed: "the cure for neuroses."

I had tried college for two years but I wasn't ready for it, at least emotionally. Another book called *The Trial* by Franz Kafka convinced me of the futility of knowledge without meaning or purpose in my life. Therefore, I quit school and thought I'd work for a while. All I found were dead ends and disappointments—an apprentice carpentry job where all the talk was anti-commie, down with Jane Fonda, and let's get to work. And later, a folk-singing gig that lifted my hopes for exactly two weeks. "Yeah. You're finished kid," I heard on the phone from the bartender, "and no you can't talk to the bosses."

Although I was being stripped of my ideal of how good man was, I still clung to man's ideas to save me. God was not an alternative. I had gone the church route with my family. I'd ushered on Sundays, poured coffee at church breakfasts, raked church leaves, washed church windows, and rang the church bell. When I was 15, my parents gave me the option if I wanted to go to church. My father even suggested that I try various ones in the area. I remember thinking, "Why go to church at all?" Church was a place for old bald-headed men who got upset at teenagers for not ringing the bell at precisely the right moment, or silver wavy-haired smiling businessmen who didn't miss a Sunday but told racist jokes when you worked around their house. No, church just demanded much and gave little.

I needed acceptance, and in high school I thought that it might come through being in a rock group, drinking with the guys, and finding a girlfriend. But, the more I pursued acceptance in these ways, the more I despised myself. Finally, I found someone who said she loved me, and she became my primary companion. Still my fears overwhelmed me, and a sense of fatalism obscured my future. When my brother offered me *The Primal Scream* to read, it seemed a last straw, and I clutched at it. So my girlfriend, Cheryl (not real name), a buddy, and I took a Trailways bus to L.A.

I called the Primal Institute in Beverly Hills the day after we found a place to stay to see when I could start therapy. The receptionist on the phone said that I was too young, and "No" I could not have a therapist explain why, if the therapy was the truth, I was being rejected. Hanging up the phone, I walked along the overpass bridge above Route 101 in Santa Monica. I leaned over the railing and was abruptly brought to my senses by the loud scream, "Jump!"

Seeing the garbage collector looking out of the truck window, waiting for me to bounce off the pavement, was enough for me to change my mind. I wasn't going to give some sadist any pleasure—not on his life or mine!

The next several months I searched for similar therapies that took in younger people. I took frequent trips to the library and bookstore and I finally discovered one. You only had to be 18. My time in therapy amounted to three months. Cheryl returned to Rhode Island to finish her degree while I flew to San Rafael. At the end of three months "getting into primals," I dimly began to realize an important truth. I could choose to hate and blame people for the rest of my life for the way I was. In fact, during a "wrap-up" group therapy session I had involuntarily raised my arms to strike a therapist when he encouraged me to vent my feelings of anger toward him. My loss of control scared me. It seemed as if this hatred was a bottomless pit.

I returned home for Christmas, Cheryl received her diploma, and we both found work to save for a return trip to California. I still needed to resolve something and Primal Therapy was all I had.

In all fairness, I must say, too, that God had been trying to get through to me the whole time I was in California. My twin brother had become a Christian while in the army and his prayer group must have been working overtime. Everywhere I went it seemed Christians had a conspiracy to "get Tim." A Salvation Army man felt compelled to give me a Bible on the bus. Another young man I sat next to wanted to talk about prayer. Every group witnessing on the beach always seemed to gravitate to me. A girl at the nursing home where I worked while going through therapy talked of being drawn to a church "to talk to God." A couple of guys came to our apartment complex to tell us about Christ. I felt very smug and said, "I don't need him." Meanwhile, despite my pretensions of "togetherness," my life was in shambles.

Then came my second trip to California. Within a couple of months after arriving, my girlfriend and I were penniless and living in our beat-up Corvair. Someone we met suggested that we call a Christian hotline. With their help, perhaps, we could find a place to stay and some food. I called but refused to accept that Cheryl and I would sleep apart. They weren't going to force their values on me! I asked if there was any way we could get food without "strings attached." I was amazed that the woman on the phone didn't argue with me. She just agreed to meet us at our location.

I readied myself for the 'Jesus rap,' but the two young women with the white waxed paper bag only asked us where we were from and where we were going. That was all right with me. I didn't have a whole lot of energy for a debate and I was extremely curious about what was in the bag. Donuts? At last they left and Cheryl and I uncovered the secrets. We never tasted such delicious apples, cheese, fresh bread, and milk in all our lives.

When it was thoroughly consumed, there was only one thing left to do—our daily routine: go to the park, break twigs, and say, "I don't know" to each other. However, on the way back from the park this time something strange was happening. A definite conflict was taking place in my mind and my thoughts ran something like this: *You're not too smart by not accepting a place to sleep. You're not sleeping with your girlfriend anyway—just getting bruises sleeping on suitcases.* Another voice seemed to take the opposite view: *Oh yeah. You tell Cheryl you want to accept their conditions and she'll think you're a hypocrite. You've been put down Christians ever since you've known her. You'll be admitting defeat.*

Ultimately, I sided with wisdom and asked Cheryl if she would mind if I called back the person on the hotline. Her enthusiastic "Yes!" surprised me. I swallowed my pride and gave them a call.

The next thing I knew, we were sitting on a couch in an apartment where Cheryl was going to stay and a young man stood in front of us preaching the love of God as revealed through Jesus Christ. I had never heard such powerful words in all my life. I had arrived at the end of my tunnel. All my attempts at obtaining peace of mind had ended at a rock wall but now it seemed a hole was being drilled through my hard heart and there was a way out. Light arose in the darkness.

A few days later a pastor explained to me the steps of salvation—that I confess my self-centeredness, turn from my way of doing things, receive Christ's forgiveness by faith and welcome Him into my life to change my heart. I humbled myself and did these things and God came into my life. Cheryl also came to Christ at the same time. We eventually saw that God wasn't leading us together to get married and so we separated.

My feelings of alienation from others changed radically. I sensed love for others that I hadn't experienced since I was a child. I felt that I belonged to a new family. I began to learn how to read the Bible and let God reveal Himself to me.

Twenty-five years have passed since that day and God is still changing me more into His image. My fatalistic view of my future has been replaced with confidence and hope. My self-loathing has changed to self-acceptance and appreciation.

In 1979, I received my BA in English Literature and in 1983 I had the privilege to go to France for three years, to work with a missionary organization called Youth With A Mission.

It was there I met a wonderful woman from Belgium named Véronique, who became my wife in 1985. We spent our first year of marriage travelling around France conducting video seminars on various aspects of the Christian life such as *How to Hear the Voice of God, Marriage and the Family, Spiritual Warfare,* and *Understanding the Father Heart of God.*

We came to the States in1986 with the idea of returning to Europe immediately to go to Bible school. God had other plans, however, and we stayed for another 14 years before going back. Some of the reasons for God's delay were obvious—we adopted our first two children, Alicia and Samuel, during that time and we also had the opportunity to learn about church leadership by serving in various capacities in our church. I also learned about pioneering by being self-employed in a vinyl and leather repair business for six years and publishing a Christian business directory for another four years. I also wrote part-time over those years and had the honor of being published in a variety of magazines and news-papers (on the cover of *Guideposts* magazine in March of 1997) and winning first prize in the national Amy Awards in 1999.

Presently, we are utilizing everything we have learned to start a church in a small city in the south of France that has never had an evangelical church in its entire history.

Not everything changed overnight for me, but through the years God has taught me to no longer see myself as a passive victim to the forces around me but as someone He can use to touch people with His love. God has proven His word to me from Jeremiah 29:11: *"For I know the plans I have for you,"* declared the Lord, *"plans to prosper you and not to harm you, plans to give you a hope and a future."*

(cont'd.)

Other verses to look up: **Romans 3:23, Romans 6:23, Romans 10: 9 & 10, Romans 10:14-15**

Do you know for certain that you are saved?

If not, why not follow the steps that I made in this last story to receive Christ into your heart. Confess that you are a sinner. Turn away from your sins. Ask Jesus to come into your heart by faith. Confess with your mouth that you believe that Jesus died for you and that God raised Him from the dead. Then follow Jesus.

Questions if you are certain of your salvation:

Do you naturally love interacting with people from different cultures and befriending them?

Do you love to travel?

Do you like learning other languages?

Would you like the challenge of living out the Gospel and sharing it with people from another nation?

Have you considered that there might be a missionary calling on your life?

To receive the Bennett family newsletter, please write:

Faith Chapel
4113 West Seneca Turnpike
Syracuse, NY 13215

If you want to support their ministry financially, please send checks addressed to:

Elim Fellowship
P.O. Box 57A
Lima, N.Y. 14485

To order Tim's books
($12 each plus shipping and sales tax where applicable):
With A Grain of Salt
Salt for the Supper Table

Contact the Elim Bookstore
E-mail: bookstore@elim.edu
Phone: (585) 624-3380 ext. 308
Mail: 7245 College Street, Lima NY 14485

For bulk orders of 10 or more, contact Elim Publishing:
E-mail: info@elimpublishing.com
Phone: (585) 624-5560
Mail: Elim Publishing, 1679 Dalton Road, Lima NY 14485

You can also write the Bennetts at:
9, Clemence et Marius Gras
Valreas, France 84600
or
timbennett5@yahoo.com